The House at the End of the Old Gravel Road

Brenda Strohbehn Henderson

To the residents of small towns
everywhere—
keep writing your history, sharing your stories,
and living your dreams

———

and to Joe ...
for all of our tomorrows

CONTENTS

PREFACE

Bitsy Lee Evans is a fictional character whose story is set in Dodgeville, South Carolina. Mrs. Evans not only shares her own story on the following pages, but she also introduces you to the residents of Dodgeville through her blog posts and live feeds over the Internet.

Bitsy's authentic and unpretentious descriptions of her hometown have earned her a large following. You'll find yourself eager to follow her as well, just to meet her friends and learn more about her quaint little town.

As you read *The House at the End of the Old Gravel Road*, you will see three formatting indicators:

Standard formatting: This indicates Bitsy's firsthand narration of her everyday life.

Indented block formatting, italics: *This indicates a blog post that Bitsy is writing for her website.*

Indented block formatting, regular font: This indicates a "live feed" that Bitsy is recording for her followers.

Dodgeville, SC
It doesn't exist, but you'll wish it did.

The Old Gravel Road Series

CHAPTER 1

"Say that again."

"Say *what* again?"

"That thing you just said to Jay about how to find our new house."

"Um, let's see. 'Friday...see you then...casual....' Oh yeah, 'We're the house at the end of the old gravel road.'" He looked at me over the bifocals that were perched on the end of his nose. "That part? Why?"

"It's what we've been looking for. It's *perfect*!"

He grinned at me as if he had intentionally spoken the magic words that had sent my mind into an easily achieved pinnacle of happiness.

I didn't take time to smile back. Instead, my joyful "I love you!" trailed off in the distance as I all but ran to my desk in the sunroom and woke up my computer. I typed the words at the top of the page, studied them for the briefest of intensely judgmental moments, and breathed an audible all-is-well sigh.

That was nine years ago this March.

CHAPTER 2

Y'all keep asking me to join the "Get-to-Know-Me Challenge," so here we go!

[It was here that I hesitated. I hoped it was a brief enough pause that it would look as if I had done it for effect. Sharing such trivial elements of my life seemed, well, trivial, and I wanted my followers to take me seriously. Yet, this "challenge" was just about to reach its peak, and I wanted to fulfill the expectations people would have...before it was "so yesterday!"]

Where am I from? I'm from all over the place. I've lived in six states—three of them, twice each. Right now I live in South Carolina. While some of my family members are shoveling snow this week, Henry and I are wearing short-sleeved T-shirts on our daily walks. We love it. I hope we're here permanently.

What's my favorite food? Macaroni and cheese. It used to be that I *only* liked the kind that came in a box. However, after tasting the mac and cheese made by Miss Pauline down at the Sweet Tea and Sunshine Café, I changed my mind. Hers is the best *anywhere*! However, I still really, really like the kind from the box, and it rates a very close second. No other recipes need apply.

[The minute I said it, I knew I'd get more private messages than I could answer that night, each containing the sender's favorite recipe for the *perfect* mac-and-cheese casserole. Too late now.]

Favorite color? Yellow. Always. Yellow is just so cheery! And don't even get me *started* on the joy that yellow roses bring!

Favorite teacher? Miss Marlowe. I didn't even stop to think about that one. She was my English teacher my senior year in high school. Though others encouraged me along the way, she's the sole reason I became a writer. She taught me to love words—their beauty, their power, their ability to paint pictures and to make dreams come true and minds more knowledgeable. She loved what she did; therefore, I realized that I loved it too!

How long have you been blogging or doing live feeds? Nine years this March. Nine...glorious...years! I began blogging soon after we moved to the house at the end of the old gravel road.

Whew—final question! **If I could change anything that happened in my past, what would it be?** Wow. That's both a terribly difficult and yet incredibly easy question to answer: Nothing. Not. One. Thing. My dad used to answer this same question that way, adding, "Each thing I did, went through, learned from, failed at, succeeded at, loved, hated brought me to right where I'm at today...and I like it here." I can say it no better than that.

And it's true. It's all true.

Clicking the button to post the brief video segments without first editing them felt vulnerable but freeing. Besides, a promise is a promise, and I had promised several of my followers that I would do it.

The video challenge, however, was a breeze compared to what I was certain to face within the next few minutes.

CHAPTER 3

I headed straight for the doctor's office—an old, yellowed-brick building where the laundromat had once stood. As I came around the corner from the parking lot, Dr. Rick Michaels, coming from Miss Pauline's café with a turkey, beef, and ham sub in one hand, held the door for me with his free one.

"He's already back in the corner room. I just got a text from Stephanie that he was here a little early."

CHAPTER 4

I'm a born storyteller. In my estimation, brief answers with no backstory or emotion are barely worth the breath it takes to speak to them.

However, for the first time in a long time, I wished for the ability to give more than a succinct, unemotional reply. Words escaped me. Doc seemed to understand my momentary lapse and silently, with only a look from his empathy-filled eyes, gave me the courage simply to breathe in and out in that moment.

"Parkinson's disease."

Just last week Henry had asked me if I had noticed how my dad's steps seemed rigid and his quick mind incapable of focusing on more than one thing at once. Mom had noticed a "droop" to his smile. Thinking back, I realized that this symptom had shown up even more in pictures than in person. I hadn't understood its presence, but it was there.

Suddenly, with nearly the urgency of someone fleeing a burning building, I needed to write. I wanted to run from the room and head home to my ever-welcoming keyboard to pour out my thoughts. The words were there, crashing into the corners of my mind as they longed for me to open the floodgate to release them. But that would have to wait. I needed to help. I needed to listen.

What I *wanted* to do was to sort through the new realities that would be ours—all of ours.

Mom was a rock. Henry was a rock. Dad—sweet, gentle, Parkinson's-riddled Dad—was a rock. I was...about to become engulfed in a puddle of tears.

I honestly don't remember what I said. It was encouraging. It was helpful. It was loving. At least that's what both Mom and Henry said.

"Should Daddy drive home?" I whispered as Henry and I walked hand in hand behind my parents, who were walking in the same manner—as they always did.

Henry nodded. "He's fine. The only thing different from an hour ago is that we have a name for what's happening." We both knew that my father *needed* to drive home—to feel as if he still had control over *something*. "As long as it's safe for him to do so, I think he should be allowed to keep driving."

Seatbelt now fastened, I asked Henry if we could pick up a turkey, beef, and ham sub from Miss P's. I didn't feel like cooking, and for some reason that I couldn't think of, that's what sounded good.

As we drove over the first pebble that greeted us

on the old gravel road, my tears were jostled out of their safekeeping.

Henry understood when I headed straight to the sunroom and began telling the story I had just been given permission to share.

CHAPTER 5

My fingers achieving the quicker route for my words to make their exit from my heart and out into the world, I decided to start with my blog post for tomorrow morning and share info via live feed after the blog's subscriber e-mail went out. Yes, since this was an out-of-the-ordinary post, I could post it tonight, but we hadn't talked with my brother yet— Allen was still working until five o'clock Central time, and I would *not* want my big brother to hear this news via a blog post, so I would schedule it to go live in the morning.

I first poured myself a cup of coffee, because I couldn't lie to my readers, and I didn't want to encourage them to have their morning coffee or tea with me and not truly have any beverage of my own to drink.

CHAPTER 6

Today I'm using one of my favorite mugs: the one with the picture of my parents talking to Henry and me on the morning of our wedding. It seemed appropriate. And soon I'll tell you why. But first, go grab your coffee or tea, and I'll meet you right back here. Don't worry if it takes a few extra minutes to brew. I'll wait...right here at the end of the old gravel road.

[Why did my standard opening suddenly seem so trite? When I started *The Old Gravel Road* nine years ago, I determined from the very first blog post that I would include my readers. They were *my* stories, yes, but their purpose focused solely on those who honored me by showing up to read the posts. Henry was actually the one who came up with the opening one morning while we were enjoying coffee and talking about some of the stories I wanted to share on the website someday. Every rule of blogging said I needed a catchier opening than the one that was now my signature line, but rules...well, I'll just politely say that my sponsors seem just fine with my opening! However, today it seemed so cliché—so pretentious. It felt as if I were looking at the words of someone whose blog I was reading for the first time.]

Henry and I have welcomed you into our home since the end of our first year of marriage. That's when we moved to this state, this town, this house. Since then, you've been there for us, and we've been there for you.

If I could invite you into our home this morning, I would—every single one of you. But I need your hugs, your prayers, and the sweet encouragements you always share with each other in the comments. The atmosphere in this circle of unmet friends is what keeps me writing. You are the reason I show up.

My dad—the dear man who is, by now, "Captain Ed" to most of you—has Parkinson's. He has most likely had it for five to ten years, and his symptoms, though few, are becoming more evident.

So why share this with thousands of men and women who don't know him personally? Because you know me, and I want to know that I can talk with you about this as we travel this road as a family—and as a blog family. In fact, my family immediately gave the go-ahead for me to share the news on this platform.

We just found out yesterday.

When plans change, when the results most likely won't be how we imagined them, when the priorities shift their focus, that's not the time to compare problems—or even solutions. I've encouraged this reaction in you—and in myself—before, but now it's time to live it.

For one brief moment I hesitated to share this. Why—when I encourage authenticity and openness in you? Because in your openly authentic ways, you have bravely shared your tragedies, disappointments, dramatic life changes, and losses. In that fleeting pause of my typing fingers I felt that my problem was not as big, not as bad, not as breathtaking, not as breath-stealing as some of yours.

And in the grand scheme, it's probably not.

But it's real to me. It's big to me. It has entered my life, though it was uninvited and in this moment is unwelcome. It is now a part of my dad's story and therefore, mine. So it will most certainly become a part of my stories both here and in my live feeds. You deserved to know what changed.

Yet in many ways, nothing has changed. We'll keep enjoying our coffee or tea together, gathered around words that unite us, make us think, and keep us moving forward. And for this, my friends, I thank you...from my desk in the sunroom...at the back of the house...at the end of the old gravel road.

CHAPTER 7

We slept surprisingly well that night. We were at peace—both with what was and with what may be.

Henry had a quick flight to England coming up on Thursday. He normally left in plenty of time to get to Charlotte before the early afternoon departure, but there was possible sleet headed into the Upstate Wednesday night, so I encouraged him to grab a room at his favorite hotel in Charlotte and leave tomorrow afternoon instead.

The hour-and-a-half drive usually gave him time to catch up on a few of his favorite podcasts or to sing along at the top of his lungs with the old Gospel Favorites station, so the frequent trips to Charlotte, his "base," were enjoyable for him. He's a pretty popular guy with the blog followers, so I enlisted his help with a little blog post early this morning.

CHAPTER 8

Every other Tuesday I volunteer at the elementary school. When Henry is in town, he comes with me and reads aloud to the first graders while I help Mrs. Markham with the tasks that would otherwise eat up her only free planning hour. I do just about everything a non-teacher can do: sharpen pencils, cut out figures or letters for her wall decor, grade spelling quizzes from a master key, organize papers to be sent home that week, and whatever else is on my Volunteer Assignment Sheet for that day. I look forward to it—almost as much as Mrs. Markham does, I'm sure!

The kids gravitate to Henry as though he were their own grandpa. It hadn't taken long for us to realize that we *were* old enough to be their grandparents, and Henry's prematurely gray hair only added to their thoughts that we were really, *really* old. Some weeks he wears his uniform and reads books about flying or tells them stories from his early years as a pilot. You can hear a pin drop as his Texas twang rings out across the carpeted reading circle in the front corner of the classroom.

He tells his stories to them, and I tell the resulting stories to my readers or post a live feed on the way home to share something cute that one of the students said. I don't use names or any specific information about the students I'm talking about. I want to protect their privacy—and mine.

CHAPTER 9

Y'all should've seen the grade one-ers today. This is apparently Spirit Week, and today they were supposed to dress up like someone in the occupation they want to have someday. There were little nurses—including one who had a fake syringe that apparently made her classmates cry when she tried to give them shots during recess!—firefighters dressed in uniforms that included boots and suspenders; teachers with schoolbooks in tow and with their hair, glasses, or clothing done in such a way so as to resemble an easily recognizable teacher or administrator at Clara McBride Elementary School; and so many more!

My favorites, however, were the four boys and two girls in Mrs. Markham's class who were dressed as airline pilots!

Henry may or may not have shed a tear...or two.

Did you ever dress up as a child for the exact career you have today? Drop me a note in the comments—and I'll even give bonus "likes" if you have a childhood photo to prove it!

We're about to turn onto the old gravel road, so I'll catch you tomorrow over on the blog!

CHAPTER 10

"Bits, do you know where my travel adapter is? I thought it was in the office, but it's not there."

"It's by your flight bag in the bonus room. I was afraid you'd forget it again, so I wanted it right there by your other things. Sorry—I should have known you wouldn't forget it twice! I'll run up and get it for you."

Henry had his system down pat, and his packing went best when I stayed out of the way. He had put in twenty-six years of travel with the airlines so far, and his preflight checklist started at home. He knew what, where, when, and how to pack. If I tried to jump in and help, it messed up the routine. So I stay busy with other things while he packs. It keeps both of us happier that way!

The surprised look on my face made Henry laugh. "How did you get up here before I did? I thought you were back in the office."

"Nah. I was already headed up to look in the suitcase when I asked you about it. I had a feeling my sweet wife had tried to help me out, so I figured it was up here. I just thought I'd double-check with you first." His smirky smile was my favorite, and today it let me know that I hadn't messed things up *too* badly!

As he folded, creased, double-checked, and then packed each item, I sat silently, thankfully, gratefully...and already planning tonight's post. But first, we headed downstairs for his favorite pre-departure lunch: egg drop soup and a corned beef sandwich. I had become an expert at making both...and enjoying only one!

CHAPTER 11

Today I'm using my "Seek New Adventures" mug. It's a gentle, almost-muted shade of turquoise, and it has an outline drawing of the prettiest little two-wheeled Victorian bike leaning against a tree. Soon you'll see why I chose this one. But first, go grab your coffee or tea, and I'll meet you right back here. Don't worry if it takes a few extra minutes to brew. I'll wait...right here at the end of the old gravel road.

Clara McBride Elementary School was all aflutter yesterday as students, dressed in their "career" attire for Spirit Week, passed fellow nurses, teachers, pilots, and firefighters in the hallway. Whispers of, "Hey, look! She wants to be a firefighter too!" and "He looks exactly like Dr. George, the science teacher in the high school!" were heard throughout the building every time there was a bathroom break or a line formed by the outside doors, headed for recess.

The good captain was with me this week, and I could tell he was honored by the six—count 'em...six!—grade one-ers dressed as mini-Henry pilots. Mrs. Markham shared with us that one of the little boys (our nearest neighbor just off of the old gravel road) had said, "Do you think Mrs. Evans might get confused and think that I'm Captain Henry? My mom says I look just like him today!"

So of course, y'all know that I had to play along. I headed over to the little one when it was time for us to leave, looped my arm through his, and said, "Well, Captain Henry, we'd better head on home and get some lunch!" He believed for a moment that he had fooled me, let out an almost melodic giggle, blushed, and then quickly removed his arm from mine! Henry gave him a thumbs-up sign, and he knew that all was well!

There's a sale on grapefruit this week over at Hendricksens' Gas and Grocery, so I need to add those to my list. I confess that I'm not a big fan of the flavor, but Mrs. Pastor Dave told me to throw some oranges in with them, and they'll taste better. My stomach isn't willing to believe her, but I love her bunches, and she's never—okay, rarely—steered me wrong, so I'll give it the old college try. After all, they're on sale!

Speaking of sweet Mrs. Pastor Dave, she dropped off some beef-barley soup for my parents today. I had planned to take them some leftover egg drop soup from our lunch and have supper with them, but since they're well cared for tonight, I think I'll just stay home, throw on my sweats, light the fire, and have some egg drop soup here at the house while I read.

Sleet is headed into the Upstate this evening, and after nine years back in the South, I've become allergic to driving on icy roads!

Have you noticed that when you stop doing something—even for a while—it's harder to do when you try again after an extended time away from that activity? The old expression, "It's like riding a bike," wasn't coined by someone who truly hadn't ridden in years. How do I know that? I don't. But I'll share a little story with you to convince you that I'm right on this one!

When Henry's gone, it's easy for me to hole up in our house here at the end of the old gravel road and forget about the world outside these walls. So I casually mentioned to him that it might be fun to get a bike that I could use to ride downtown and visit friends. Trust me, I had no real desire to get a bike.

However, y'all know my dear Henry. Next thing I knew, he had gone down to Anderson and Sons Hardware and had asked Denny to order a bike that had all the bells and whistles on it.

WAIT! (Yes, I just screamed that out loud in an empty house. You should have seen Wilbur jump and heard him bark! Oh, that dog!) I sometimes forget in the midst of my stories that some of y'all don't know the expressions we aging gals use to describe things. So, no, the bike did not literally have bells and whistles attached to it! That just means that it had all the "extras" it could have and still qualify as a bike.

(I'm literally laughing out loud now— once again frightening poor Wilbur— picturing my beautiful bike dripping with cowbells of varying sizes and shapes and sporting air-pumped whistle-makers on the handlebars!)

Now, where was I? Ah, yes. I was philosophizing on forgetting how to do what we no longer do.

So here I am on this brand-new bike that is a vibrant shade of a cross between magenta and coral, making it easily seen and instantly recognizable by one and all. I climb aboard the seat (which is clearly now made in a much, much, much narrower design), plant my tookus on said seat, grab the handlebars (laden with gears, brakes, and something that will tell me my current pulse rate if I ask it to), and head off to ride in circles around the two-car garage.

It wasn't pretty, friends. It was not *pretty.*

I wobbled. Then I couldn't get the pedals to move before I began to wobble again, this time with a little more wobble to the wobble.

"I'll try it later when it's not raining and I have a little more room to move around outside *the garage." I didn't want Henry to feel bad, but I also didn't want even the dearest of husbands to witness my uncomfortable wobblefest.*

Knowing that my "center of gravity" was in a new location, Henry tried his best to reassure me: "It'll come back to you soon." He also understood when it didn't.

Four months later we sold the bike at an incredible discount to a college girl over in Glenbrook. Her parents dropped her off to pick it up, and she rode the bike home—all twelve miles. Showoff!

So the point is this: It's a new season of life. Maybe "getting back on the bike" isn't a part of this new season for me.

Maybe what you used to do was what you were supposed to do then. *Maybe* now *you're equipped for something different. Or maybe you're supposed to return to the bike and better your best. Thoughts?*

Whatever you do, keep moving forward. And remember that your comments to these posts keep me *moving forward—and for this, my friends, I thank you...from my desk in the sunroom...at the back of the house...at the end of the old gravel road.*

CHAPTER 12

The forecast had been accurate: the sleet covered the trees and the roadways, making it a perfect "jammie day." However, doing an early morning live feed served as the impetus for getting out of bed, getting cleaned up and dressed, taking Wilbur for a quick, slippery walk down to the end of the old gravel road and back, and putting on at least a minimal amount of makeup.

I checked on Mom and Dad first to make sure they still had electricity. I knew they'd be up, so an early call wouldn't wake them.

"Would you have time to help me hang those photos of the boys later today? You arranged the other ones so nicely that I'd be afraid of messing up the flow if I tried to do it myself." Mom was a great decorator; she just needed reassurance—or another person to talk to.

We established a good time for me to stop by, talked about our breakfast menus, and hung up with our standard exchange of, "I love you."

I headed to my filming spot in the sunroom after grabbing my new mug and filling it with some snickerdoodle coffee I had picked up down at Hendricksens' G and G last week.

CHAPTER 13

My blog post yesterday was longer than some. But who can relate to that bike story? I woke up wondering if I still had the number of that girl in Glenbrook, thinking I might call her to see if she would want to sell the bike back to me so that I could try riding it just one more time.

Then Wilbur barked; I came to my senses; and I started my day in the glorious realities of the here and now.

First Thursday of the month, so it's "Thankful Thursday." I'll start.

I'm thankful for a warm house, hot coffee, and the promise of sweet tea on the porch in only a month or so! How about you? Drop your gratitude list in the comment bar, and we'll even draw a name from the entries. If Henry draws your name on Saturday night when the entry period ends (at 5:00 p.m., Eastern time), you'll get a mug with "The Old Gravel Road" logo from our website!

Now, let's share some gratitude, y'all!

CHAPTER 14

"I don't think we need anything other than an oil change, Junior. Oh wait. Henry did mention that he had called you about those annoying wipers. Do you mind checking those too? That screeching sound is about to cause us to trade this car in for a new one." Before he could open his mouth to see if he could "interest me in a new car today," I asked about Jillian, whom everyone in Dodgeville knew to ask about whenever Fred Liddle was trying to get you to buy a new car before you were ready to do so: "How's Jill doing these days?"

"I think the big city has captured her heart."

"And I'm certain she has captured the hearts of the people there. She's a gem, that girl of yours. Sweet as can be. Now, shall I pick up the car at a set time this afternoon, or do you just want to give me a call when it's done?"

"Oh, I'll just drop it by your house on my way home. Jeff is working with me today, framing some new art pieces for the show, so he'll follow me and give me a ride the rest of the way. You going to be home?"

"I'm headed to my parents' house for a bit to help Mom hang some new family photos, so I guess you actually could just drop it by there, since that's right on your way. If you need to keep it overnight, just let me know, and I'll have Dad drop me back at the house."

"Speaking of your dad, how's the good captain doing these days? Still able to drive okay?"

"Aw, thanks for asking about him, Junior. He's still able to drive, and we're grateful for that. But he's learning that we all have limitations—even him! He's getting in a few more naps at Mom's insistence, and Doc Michaels says that's a good thing for his Parkinson's."

"He a good man, Bitsy. He's been one of my best customers since I took over the dealership over twenty-five years ago at the ripe old age of twenty. He's an encourager and one loyal fella. I've always liked him. We said a little prayer for him at dinner the night we read your post about his Parkinson's. Give him and your mom my best. Maybe I'll stop in and say howdy when I drop your car off. Would that be okay?"

CHAPTER 15

Stop it right now. They recently got "I [heart] Dodgeville" mugs down at the Sweet Tea and Sunshine Café (aka, Miss P's), and I just had to have one! Apparently, Fred Liddle designed the artwork for them, and they are amazing! So yep, that's the mug I'm drinking my coffee from this morning. Y'all have met so many of our sweet townspeople through this blog, and I know I've told you a lot about Miss Pauline and her incomparable macaroni and cheese; however, I still need to introduce you to Fred Liddle. But first, go grab your coffee or tea, and I'll meet you right back here. Don't worry if it takes a few extra minutes to brew. I'll wait...right here at the end of the old gravel road.

Fred Liddle is an old soul. He thinks, talks, acts much older than his forty-some-odd years. He's smart as a whip, funny, carefree, and as talented as they come. But more than all of that, he's loyal to Dodgeville. It's been good to him, and he's been good to the town.

His wife is this adorable petite traffic-stopper with a smile that made me smile just now even thinking about it. Katy works over at Miss P's, and Miss Pauline always introduces her to customers by saying, "And this is Katy. She puts the sunshine in 'Sweet Tea and Sunshine,' even though I didn't name my café after her. Now, can we get you a big glass or a little glass of sweet tea today?"

Katy and Fred met at the University of South Carolina their freshman year. Back then, Katy had long hair and wore it in a ponytailed version of a messy bun—every day. She stood out in sharp contrast to the well-groomed preppy classmates she shared a major with. She was one of those think-outside-the-box kind of marketing majors, and Fred was instantly drawn to her equal blend of creativity and brilliance. She had her heart set on taking the marketing world by storm in Chicago (her hometown) after graduation, and anyone who knew her had no doubt that she would achieve that goal.

Fred, though blessed with the same key strengths, would be described in the reverse order from Katy: brilliant and creative. He had an eye for business and also design, leading to his ultimate goal of heading first to New York and then somewhere in Europe—he had not yet pinpointed the exact where—to oversee acquisitions for an art gallery. His double major in art history and marketing were uniquely blended into the perfect formula for his path to future success.

A Dodgeville boy from birth, Fred pretty much knew everyone in town. Perhaps it was his own eye for beauty or perhaps it was his mother's artistic ability and genuine Southern charm that influenced him so deeply, but he saw the good—no, he looked for the good—in everything and everyone. His eyes spoke to you before he opened his mouth: "You matter; it'll be okay; I'm glad I know you; I'm here—I'm your friend." And when they finished flashing their welcoming, gentle message your way, you believed them. And you found yourself loving Fred.

Oh friends, I have so much more to tell you about this dear man, but I need to head to my parents' house and arrange family photos on the gallery wall. Please come back tomorrow so that I can tell you more about the last place you would have expected to find Fred Liddle.

You are always so patient when I leave you hanging, and for this, my friends, I thank you...from my desk in the sunroom...at the back of the house...at the end of the old gravel road.

CHAPTER 16

"Mom, what was Fred Liddle's mom's name? For the life of me, I just can't remember it!"

"Hi, Mom! Hi, Dad! How are *you* doing this afternoon?" Even her sarcasm was sweetly spoken as she tried to help me remove my jacket, which somehow had gotten tangled around the purse strap that was supported by my right wrist. She pulled. I pulled. We both laughed as I clumsily apologized for not properly greeting them on my way into the house.

"No problem, Bitsy, dear." She walked to the stairwell to drop my jacket over the crook at the end of the banister. "Josie. Her name was Josie."

When I looked at Dad today, I thought, *You'd never know there was any kind of disease attacking his body. He looks as healthy as Henry.* He had none of the stereotypical symptoms associated with Parkinson's: no tremors, shaking, or sudden, involuntary twitch-like movements. Instead, my dad's Parkinson's manifested more in rigidity, slower thought processes, and that downward droop to his now sometimes slightly drooling mouth.

"Why are you asking about Josie Liddle, dear one?" Dad's voice rang out nice and strong from the other side of the great room.

"I'm telling Fred's story in a blog post that already has turned into a *few* blog posts. He's allowing me to share the entire story."

Several moments of silence followed, as each of us seemed to feel that the trivialities of today may somehow throw a blanket of disrespect over the event just remembered.

Mom's gentle sigh not only broke the silence but changed the subject: "Well, dear, we need to get these photos up before Fred drops your car off. I imagine you have a to-do list a mile long of things you want to accomplish while Henry's out. I know I always made lists when your dad had an overseas trip. They were usually more for the purpose of keeping my mind busy than about the things that got done. It sort of made it a win-win to add a checkmark next to something before heading to bed."

We both looked over and saw Dad already dozing in his recliner. After exchanging knowing glances that said, "Let's not wake him," Mom whispered, "I may start making those to-do lists again. Your father needs to feel a sense of accomplishment at the end of the day. I think he's feeling a little useless lately. Now, where shall we put these new photos?"

CHAPTER 17

As I often did when sharing a two- or three-part story, I omitted the standard opening for the next blog post about Fred. I jumped right back into it and assumed that the readers would either already have read part one or would feel compelled to go back and read it after enjoying today's post. If there was one thing I'd learned after nearly nine years of blogging, it was that readers deserved more credit than we bloggers often gave them. They were smart, and the style in which we wrote should reflect our respect for them.

> *Katy first visited Dodgeville the summer after their freshman year. Fred, Sr. and Josie knew right away that there was no better match for their son. Despite being a big-city girl, she fit right in and saw the beauty in both the landscape and the people of their little town. For Fred, Jr. and Katy, despite their relatively young age, it wasn't a matter of if, but when.*
>
> *Both Freds were taking flying lessons at the downtown airport in Greenville that summer. Fred, Sr. enjoyed a head start by getting his course work done while his son was in school over in Columbia. Fred, Jr.'s plan was to get in as many hours of flying as possible that summer so that he would have his private pilot's*

license before Thanksgiving. That's when he could finally take Katy flying alone, without the instructor in the right seat, and that's when he would propose to her.

By Thanksgiving Day, Katy had flown with Fred so often that she truly had no clue that anything was different about this flight, other than that no instructor was needed this time. Fred's spot-on landing positioned them just inches from where his mom and aunt had been instructed to place the red-carpet runner. With her attention diverted by the usual post-flight routine inside the plane, and because of Fred's skillfully angled parking of the plane, Katy did not and could not see the red carpet. Additionally, she was unaware of the little, round, beautifully decorated table for two—and matching wrought-iron chairs—that Fred, Sr. and Mikey G (the flight school's maintenance manager) had carried from the hangar and had set at the end of the red carpet.

While the men placed the table and chairs with the same precision that they had practiced numerous times the last two weeks, Josie ran into the hangar to get the bouquet of flowers and cake that she had prepared earlier that morning. With the final task complete, the four ran back into the hangar, got out their cameras and camcorders, and prepared to capture the event through videos and pictures, based on the particular medium Fred had assigned to them.

The sun was just setting in the west, and Fred's meticulously timed schedule went off without a hitch! (He had carried the ring in his pocket the entire day, his only fear having been that he—or someone else—would forget to bring it to the airport.)

To this day, when Katy speaks of her shock at seeing the red carpet when she rounded the back of the plane that day, she gets a little misty-eyed. "It was one for the books, that's for sure." She quickly adds, "Oh, and I said yes!"

Well, friends, my two-parter is about to become a three-parter...or perhaps even four, because this story deserves more than a quick wrap-up. You frequently ask me to include "even more of the fun details," and for this, my friends, I thank you (and I shall do it)...from my desk in the sunroom...at the back of the house...at the end of the old gravel road.

CHAPTER 18

"Wilbur, kennel." I waited. "Seriously, Wilbur, I mean it. Kennel." Would he *ever* heed my commands? This was the question I asked myself nearly every Sunday as I attempted to get our adorably stubborn—stubbornly adorable?—pup into his crate before we headed to the service at Dodgeville Community Church.

"So Wilbur still refuses to get in his cage, huh?" Pastor Dave laughed as we scurried, obviously frazzled, through the large double doors that led into the auditorium, looked for Mom and Dad, and headed down the side aisle to sit next to them in the pew. We were there just long enough to exchange howdies, grab an order of service from the rack attached to the pew in front of us, and stand back up when Pastor Tim stood to lead us in the opening prayer.

"I'm just resting my eyes," Henry whispered in reply to my second elbow nudge during the sermon.

"It must be some jet lag this morning," was his response to the third one.

Pastor Dave was a great orator of lessons from the Bible, so it wasn't that my poor Henry was bored. He was just plum tuckered out. And who could blame him? I doubt anyone else at DCC that morning had just returned from a three-day trip—

to London! Nor would they know that he had. Dear Henry was humble, and he knew that after the textile mill in Glenbrook had closed all those years ago, the economy of both Dodgeville and Glenbrook remained in a perpetual flux. Not everyone understood that Henry's travels were not exotic "free" getaways; they were hard work, and they were his livelihood. We generally kept information about his schedule off of our social media platforms.

"We won't stay long this afternoon, Mom. Henry's pretty whooped from his trip this week, so we'll probably do the 'eat and run' thing today, okay? I'm going to swing by the house to let Wilbur out and grab the salad from the fridge, so Henry will ride with you and Dad if that's okay. I'll be there soon!"

We had both parked in our usual spots—under the jittery fan-shaped branches of the large palmetto tree in the southwest corner of the unpaved lot. Henry circled around behind the car to lean in my driver's-side window and give me a quick kiss.

"See you soon, sweet Beulah Lee. I love you!" I giggled at his use of my legal name. In spite of my love for my great-grandmother and my disdain for being the recipient of such an outdated and "uncool" name, it always seemed to possess a delightful uniqueness when Henry spoke the words.

"Right back at ya, Cap'n Henry!" And with that, we each headed to the same location—I, with a brief detour down the old gravel road.

CHAPTER 19

For those who are new to following the live feeds, you should know that my husband is an international airline captain, as was my father before he retired a few years ago. One question that I've heard people ask both of them through the years is whether or not they get to do a lot of sightseeing while they travel.

Since these men are two of my favorite residents of Dodgeville, I thought it would be fun today to highlight a little bit of what they do on a trip. We haven't done this in a while, with both of us here at the same time, but today I asked Henry to join me! This will be a lot longer than normal, but since we're covering a little deeper story on the blog right now, I hope this will be a nice break.

Bitsy: First of all, what is your favorite country to fly to—and why?

Henry: England. I love history and old bookstores, and both of those abound in England.

Bitsy: So describe your timeline for a typical trip to England.

Henry: The trip takes place over the course of three days. On the first day, obviously, we fly over to England.

Bitsy: Let me stop you already. How long is that flight?

Henry: The flight itself, out of Charlotte, is about seven hours, and it always leaves in the evening. The flight is nonstop and lands at London's Heathrow Airport around six or seven in the morning, their time.

Bitsy: Thanks for adding that.

Henry: The distance is about four thousand miles. For this flight to England, I fly an Airbus A-330, twin-engine, intercontinental jet. It carries 264 passengers, has a crew of thirteen, and has a maximum gross takeoff weight of over five hundred thousand pounds.

Bitsy: To this day, I still have no clue how something that heavy ever gets off the ground! Next question: Walk us through what happens after you leave the airport in London.

Henry: The airline arranges for a large bus to pick us up and take us directly to the hotel they have booked for us. In London, it's usually downtown, about thirty to forty-five minutes from the airport. After they drop us off, we check in and confirm our departure pickup time for the next day.

Bitsy: So you have the whole day in London, right? I'm sure many will want to know if you simply head to your room and sleep for the next twenty-four hours (since you flew all night), or if you take off and go sightseeing.

Henry: After a shower, I generally head to bed and set my alarm for midafternoon, local time, to get up. At that point....

Bitsy: Let me interrupt again. Do you eat before you go to bed? It seems like your meal schedule would be all messed up.

Henry: No, I don't eat anything then, because I've had a meal on the plane overnight and have already had breakfast on the plane. So there's no need to eat again. Now, where was I? Oh, yes, I had just woken up! So after I wake up, I choose a landmark, museum, walking path, or point of interest to visit. I try to choose places that are within walking distance from the hotel so that I can get some exercise while I'm there. After I do my sightseeing—so now it's early evening (roughly six o'clock their time)—I find a place to have dinner.

Bitsy: Do you prefer to try local specialties or play it safe with American food?

Henry: I personally like the local specialty items. In England, that includes things like fish and chips, and as you know (since we had some on our last visit), they have really good steaks there. For some reason, they serve a lot of peas, so it seems that just about every meal comes with a side of peas. The British locals eat the peas with their knife. It's fun to watch!

Bitsy: No wonder you prefer green beans over peas when I offer them here! So what's next on a typical trip?

Henry: After dinner is when I like to visit the bookstores and old libraries. And that's when I do most of my reading. [My Henry is a voracious reader!] Eating the meal, combined with the additional time of walking to the stores and other sites, starts to tire me out, so I generally head back to bed around ten o'clock their time, nice and sleepy. I set my alarm for seven o'clock the following morning. I always schedule a wake-up call with an employee at the front desk of the hotel. My travel alarm is actually the backup to their call, rather than the other way around.

Bitsy: Do you eat breakfast before you head back to the airport, or do you wait and eat on the plane?

Henry: That's a good question, but I eat at the hotel. It's usually a British breakfast: baked beans, stewed tomatoes, scrambled eggs, bacon, hash browns, and some kind of toast or bread. Their sausage, quite honestly, smells awful, and it's rather bland, so I skip that, and I'd advise others to do the same. It sounds like a big breakfast, and it is. I top it off with a cup of coffee, and I'm good to go.

Bitsy: When does your flight leave London?

Henry: We generally leave around nine or ten o'clock their time. It will take us around seven hours to get home, so we'll arrive late afternoon in Charlotte. I can usually catch a flight from Charlotte to Greenville on the next possible flight, so that gets me home to Dodgeville mid to late evening.

Bitsy: I already know the answer to this one, but I think readers will want to know if you're able to adjust back to Eastern time and fall asleep easily the night you return.

Henry: Pretty much. But as you well know, Bitsy, it takes me about a day to get over the trip. In other words, I don't plan anything major on that first day home. You know I say it often, but I honestly think I have the best job in the world!

And now, my friends, you can see why Captain Henry Evans is so good at what he does. He eats, breathes, and sleeps all things aviation, yet he manages to be a great husband, father, and grandfather!

We wish it were possible for all of you to join us on a flight sometime, but for now, I'll just keep sharing our stories from my desk in the sunroom...at the back of the house...at the end of the old gravel road.

CHAPTER 20

Fred and Katy were married the next summer—following their sophomore year of college. They each turned twenty that May, and on June twenty-first, joined by friends and family from Chicago and Dodgeville, roommates from USC, officiants from their respective churches in Illinois and South Carolina, and a very pregnant groom's mother, they were married next to the gazebo in the large backyard of Dodgeville Community Church. Though Dodgeville would likely not be their home when they graduated with their marketing degrees in two years, it was where they were engaged and where they chose to hold their ceremony.

As for the "very pregnant" groom's mother, most people in town still believe that the excitement of the day was what brought on her contractions just as the bride and groom were cutting the ceremonial cake. Thankfully, due to a frighteningly speedy delivery and the brevity of the early afternoon ceremony and light hors d'oeuvre reception, the bride and groom were able to meet his "surprise sister" before heading up to Charlotte for their late-morning flight to

Colorado the next day, where they would spend ten glorious days together.

Josie spent the next few months apologizing to Fred, Jr. and Katy for little Jillian's abrupt entry on their special day. They must have reassured her hundreds of times that they were honored by her desire to be a part of their wedding day! Though they had moved into their small rental home just outside Columbia following their return from hiking and camping in Colorado, they made the hour-long trip to Dodgeville at least once a week to love on little "Jill-ba-dill" (as Katy lovingly called her) and to help get some meals into the freezer for Josie to use during the busy months that were certain to come with a newborn in the house.

Josie, a healthy and vibrant forty-three-year-old mom of a newly married son and a baby daughter, was well organized and surprisingly at ease with this major change in their household. Fred, Sr. was busy as owner and manager of the larger of the two car dealerships in town (the other belonging to Mr. Hughes, who more ran his lot as a side business now that he was retired). This left the new dad little time to help *with the baby during the day, so he willingly and lovingly got up with Jillian in the night, held her while he rocked her in the big white rocker (which was located next to one of many windows in her room), sang her familiar tunes for which he changed the words to include her name in them somewhere, and fed her from a bottle that Josie had prepared earlier that day.*

When "Junior" and Katy started their classes again that fall, they continued to schedule weekly visits to Dodgeville, usually returning to Columbia after the Sunday morning service at Dodgeville Community Church and a traditional Sunday dinner of pot roast, carrots, potatoes, and onions that had reached just the right level of yummy in the crock pot to be consumed within minutes of the Liddle family arriving home from church.

Josie and Katy both said that their time of preparing the Sunday noon meal and setting the dining room table on Saturday night was a high point of their week. That's when they could "girl talk," and the love between them was visible in their shared laughter, tears, and general conversation.

Fred, Sr. arranged for Junior and Katy to come stay with nearly four-month-old Jillian for a day so that he could give Josie a much-needed getaway to see the beautiful mountains of Virginia at the peak of their October color change. He had enjoyed his flying so much that he had recently purchased a little four-seater Cessna 172 so that he could treat some of his VIP clients to breakfast just outside of Charlotte. Now it was Josie's turn to enjoy the breakfast that had long been named by pilots as the "hundred-dollar breakfast," so named because although the meal itself was regular price, the cost to fly there was a hundred dollars (or sometimes more)!

Fred and Josie would take a round-robin-style trip, first stopping at the café near the airport in Charlotte. Next, they would head up to Virginia for what promised to be a breathtaking aerial view of the colorful Shenandoah Mountains and catch a similar view of the Blue Ridge Mountains on their return trip.

It was Josie's first time away from Jillian, and as many new mothers are apt to do, she had lists, emergency numbers, schedules, and little hand-

drawn maps that were labeled with the location of everything they would need in the baby's room. She acknowledged that perhaps she had gone a little overboard in her preparation— especially since her babysitters were her son and daughter-in-law—but she felt better knowing that everything would be okay.

Are you willing to wait for one final installment? Your comments, direct messages, and e-mails have shown such love for the Liddle family already, and for this, I thank you...from my desk in the sunroom...at the back of the house...at the end of the old gravel road.

CHAPTER 21

"I have an idea." Rarely did I give Henry enough time to fully wake from his afternoon nap before announcing some plan I had come up with while he was resting. He often joked that those four words generally meant one of two things: we were either going to buy something, or we were going to rearrange something!

Today, my idea was to DIY a project in the bonus room, which was over our garage. We had turned the south wing of the upstairs into a guest suite, and the bonus room fell directly in between the guest suite and Henry's office. It was an extremely large room, and we had game tables, my craft space, two couches, and a desk, all strategically placed throughout the room to allow for both quiet zones and conversational settings. I hadn't wanted to put too much on the walls up there, so the furniture actually provided most of the décor.

However, today I had watched a live feed from a very skilled DIYer friend who had made her project look so easy. My idea? I was certain we could create built-in bunk beds in the existing nook of the bonus room, thereby giving our twin grandgirls a fun space to read and sleep in when they came to visit. That would free up the bedroom in the guest suite where the twin beds currently were. Once we moved the beds out, we could turn that room into a guest office so that whoever was visiting could use it as a home office while they were here.

"You almost always have to give up your office when the one of the boys is here, and when we have everyone here at the same time, the girls always end up sleeping on the floor in the bonus room. So...ooh...what if we got another queen bed for the twin-bed room, moved the twin beds to a built-in bunk bed in the bonus room, and then...."

"The short answer is, 'Um...no.' The long answer is, 'Have we met? Are you actually picturing me doing a DIY project that involves building something?' Designing spaces is one thing, Bitsy. Making them happen without spending hundreds of dollars and making fourteen trips to Anderson and Sons' Hardware is something completely different! Maybe we can come up with something that utilizes what we already have."

He was right. I knew it. He knew it. I smiled, sighed my, *Well, maybe someday*, sigh, and headed to the porch to read the next article in the magazine that had arrived yesterday. Henry went back to sleep. His flight yesterday was a crazy one, thanks to wintery weather in the northeast, and he needed the extra time to rest today.

CHAPTER 22

One of the questions most often asked about my blog, *The Old Gravel Road*, is whether or not the residents of Dodgeville are okay with our telling their stories. Actually, the most frequently asked question is whether or not the residents of Dodgeville are real. The answer to both is yes...sort of.

The question about their existence gets a resounding yes. I fell in love with this town as a child and again as an adult, and these are my people—my very real neighbors, friends, and family members.

As to their consent, I will simply share that if I *don't* have their consent, you won't hear about them.

There's a genuine sense of community in our little town, and the residents of Dodgeville trust me to tell their stories truthfully, carefully, and lovingly. I'm loyal to them, and they know it. Yes, I have a few families who have asked not to be featured or mentioned on the blog— not even by a casual reference to them. One of them is a very dear friend who just prefers the safety and comfort of anonymity. I promised her that I will honor that, respect that, and adhere to that. Always have. Always will.

I share the truth, but I don't share the bad things about anyone's character or past actions. I tell their stories with a keyboard, not a paintbrush.

I'm currently telling a difficult story about one of the well-known and well-liked families in our town. Because of the seriousness of this particular story, I asked for their consent. They willingly gave it and said the same thing the others in town have said on such occasions: "We trust you, Bitsy."

My desire in the way that I tell their stories and in the reason behind my telling their stories is that those of you who watch the updates here on the live feed and those who read the blog posts can say the same thing: "We trust you, Bitsy."

CHAPTER 23

The porch, the kitchen, and the sunroom were the only three places in the house where I would record my live feeds. For Henry, and for me, the rest of our home was our haven—a safe place that wouldn't and couldn't be analyzed, critiqued, or talked about by our viewers. Most had sweet comments and pure motives in joining in, but we needed to have safeguards in place for those who may not fall into those categories—now or in the future.

The back patio was one of our "unpublished" zones. Just off the sunroom, this small slab of concrete held our grill, a couple of one-person benches, two chairs for reading, and a large round wrought-iron table with four matching chairs.

And when I say large, I mean large. That's how it looked out on our small patio, anyhow. In reality, it was only forty-seven inches in diameter, but the chairs were nothing short of sprawling in their design. The set consumed most of the prime real estate out there.

For the past nine summers we've eaten numerous meals on the patio. Henry loves to grill, and we both enjoy having our coffee outside while we read. It's just one of the many reasons that we enjoy the fact that South Carolina provides great weather to be outdoors quite often.

For the past nine summers we've said, "We don't like this table. It's just takes up too much room."

For the past nine summers we've said, "Someday we really need to get a new dining table and chairs that won't devour nearly every inch of our outdoor living space."

"Henry, I have an idea." Long story short, Andersons' Hardware was running an early spring sale on outdoor furniture to make room for all of the new sets coming in, and we now have a new table and chairs coming on Saturday! Denny said he and the boys could just drop it by our house in the morning.

That was all Henry needed to hear to say, "Let's do it!"

Sometimes new ideas are nothing more than finding the motivation and courage to carry out the old ones—well, that and a good bargain!

CHAPTER 24

Fred, Jr. clearly got his artistic skills from his mother. Josie took hundreds of pictures of the foliage that day, each the work of a photojournalist whose training enabled her to take breathtaking photos—and whose love of life and the beauty within it allowed her to capture moments and the memories that would result from them.

Her last photo of the day contained nearly as much color and beauty as the aerial shots she had taken throughout their flight. She snapped this picture as they were heading across the parking lot to their car. Looking back toward the plane, now properly tied down in its assigned spot on the parking ramp, Josie saw the setting sun hitting the side of the plane, with its brilliant colors reflected in their vibrant hues of coral, orange, fuchsia, and an almost lavender shade of periwinkle. It was stunning, and she captured it with perfection.

"I was hoping not to talk to the answering machine, but that probably means you're getting Baby Jill to bed right on time. This was a perfect day. I can't wait to show you all the photos I

took. I think my favorite was the last one—of the sunset reflecting off the plane. My heart is full. Love y'all bunches."

That was the last voice message Fred, Jr., Katy, and baby Jillian would ever receive from his parents.

Sherriff Lehman said that the other driver had lost control, and it appeared that she had somehow hit the gas pedal instead of the brake. Fred and Josie had died instantly. There were no survivors in either car. Seven lives—seven casualties.

That was nearly twenty-five years ago, if memory serves me correctly.

Jillian lives in Columbia, where she works as a physical therapy assistant at one of the large hospitals there. At her graduation celebration, she recounted, with genuine gratitude, how Fred, Jr. had dropped out of college to run the family's car dealership after her parents' deaths, just so that he could provide a good home for Katy and Jillian.

She had tearfully thanked Katy for not only being her fun sister-in-law but also her loving mother-figure: guiding Jillian, teaching Jillian, and accepting the position that had been thrust upon her but that she had accepted with inestimable grace.

There were many tears after that portion of her speech to the crowd that had gathered to celebrate her achievements.

As she dried her own tears, she graciously segued into the lighter portion of the story, in which she shared Fred, Jr.'s unique ability to combine his love for art and his skills in marketing to create what is perhaps the only car dealership/art gallery in existence. With Katy's clever creativity and quick mind as part of his marketing team, Junior had turned what was certainly a difficult and disappointing time into what he now calls "a redirecting of his dreams."

So next time you're in Dodgeville, be sure to stop by Liddle's Car Gallery and browse the beautiful cars in the lot and the extraordinary artwork in the showroom. As Fred often says, "Some come for a car and leave with a piece of art. Some come for the art and leave the lot in a new car. Some come just to see this unusual place! No matter what they come for, our goal is that they leave happy, refreshed, and encouraged. And with Katy's help, that's the goal I think we achieve!"

Oh, and while you're in the showroom, be sure to take time to view the large, elegantly framed photograph of a South Carolina sunset reflecting off of a small plane. The photo hangs just outside Fred's office. The inscription, on a small gold nameplate, reads: "This was a perfect day...my heart is full." In small print below that are the words, "Not for sale."

You have loved my little town well, and for this, my friends, I thank you...from my desk in the sunroom...at the back of the house...at the end of the old gravel road.

CHAPTER 25

A young woman I had never seen before was standing on the other side of the storm door, and Wilbur and I were both a little leery of inviting her in. I left the outer door closed and used my "business" voice, rather than my sweeter, as Henry calls it, "howdy, y'all" voice. Henry was up in his study, and I had just assumed that the ringing doorbell indicated that the box containing our new pillows for our patio was sitting outside the door, left there by a delivery driver.

After the incident two years ago with an overzealous blog follower showing up at the front door with a thermos of coffee in one hand and her favorite mug in the other, I've practiced a little extra caution. In fact, I removed the "come join me for a cup of coffee" that used to be in the opening to each post. I tweaked it a bit so that it no longer sounds like I'm literally inviting people I don't know to stop by the house anytime they choose!

Bless her heart, she loved our little town and its people so much that when she found our house—at the end of the old gravel road—she went back to her hotel room in Glenbrook, grabbed a thermos of coffee, and headed over to take me up on my "sweet offer!"

That incident ended well, but it had served as the impetus for installing our current alarm system—something rarely seen or used in Dodgeville prior to that time.

"Your mom said you should call her before you open the door to me. She sent me, but she didn't have time to call you before I would get here." Her rapidly spoken announcement took me off guard.

Did she just tell me to call my mom before letting her in? Whoa. Back space, lady. "I'm sorry. I didn't catch what you said. Will you please repeat that?"

She now spoke in *such* a slow manner that it made me inwardly giggle: "I just came...from your mom's house. She sent me...to see you...but she knows that you don't...know me. However, she didn't have time...to call you first, so she wants you...to call her...before you let me in. Go ahead. I'll just...wait out here...if that's okay with you. You have...a lovely porch...by the way."

"Henry, will you please come get *Orville*?" I called up the stairs, not actually for assistance with Wilbur but to have Henry nearby in case something weird was about to happen.

"Coming." I knew that he'd understood my code word, and I began to feel safer already. While reminiscing recently about that visit from the coffee-thermos woman, we had decided to come up with a word that would imply the need for instant help if the situation ever arose. I was to call our Wright-brothers-named puppy, Wilbur, by the name of the other Wright brother, Orville. Today, I was grateful that it had worked!

Henry had bounded down those stairs so quickly that I barely had my index finger ready to press Mom's contact information before he was standing next to me.

"You okay?" He leaned in close enough for me to hear and took hold of Wilbur's collar as if heeding my request for help with the dog.

"I think so. Listen in while I call Mom."

"You're calling your mom? Right now? But I thought that someone...."

"Hi, Mom. Will you please explain to me why there is a woman standing at my front door telling me to call you?"

Henry glanced in the direction of the door.

"There's no reason to speak in such scolding tones, dear. You're safe. She's from the design firm in Greenville that gave away a room makeover you didn't bother to sign up for that time we were downtown at that cute little restaurant there. Remember—the one with the stone exterior and that delicious hot chicken salad that you and Henry like to eat at when you go to downtown Greenville? Which reminds me, were you able to get that recipe from the...?"

"Mom! There is a woman I don't know standing outside my door! Maybe we could catch up on small talk later! Please...just tell me who she is!"

"Well, I won that contest! No, that's not exactly right. *You* won that contest! I entered your name on the card I filled out, and you *won*! You get a free room makeover! Let her in—right now!"

CHAPTER 26

"I can understand your hesitation, Mrs. Evans."

"Please, call me Bitsy—everyone does."

"Okay...Bitsy. I would be skeptical too if someone showed up on my front doorstep to tell me I had won a contest I had never entered. We had all of your mother's contact information on the entry card she submitted, so that's why we went to *her* house first. The signed entry gave us permission to surprise the winner at home and take photos of the room to make over."

"But I'm not at that address, so does that invalidate my...um, her...our winning the room makeover?"

"Not at all. Your mom was wise to include your name as the 'gift entrant,' which was an option we provided this time. So it's 100 percent legit. Congratulations, Bitsy and ...." She reached out to shake Henry's hand.

"I'm sorry. In my surprise, I neglected to introduce my husband. Henry, this is Molly. Molly...my husband, Henry."

"Well, Miss Molly, it's a pleasure to meet you— especially under *these* circumstances. Thank you for your patience with us."

"The pleasure is mine, Henry. Now, if you two would allow me to bring some hot chicken salad from your favorite little restaurant in Greenville next Tuesday, say, around 11:30—yes, your mom told me it's your favorite!—we can discuss the specifics and the timing for your all-expenses-paid room makeover. That will give you time to choose which room you want to do and will give me a chance to look at the room and get started on some ideas." She looked over at me, and I knew that my eyes had given me away. "You're already thinking about the room, aren't you, Bitsy?"

"Well actually, I have an idea...starting with this: Could we meet you for lunch at the Sweet Tea and Sunshine Café downtown instead?"

Henry knew right away what I was thinking. He nodded his head in knowing agreement. "I like it. Great idea, Bits."

Poor Molly had no idea what she was about to get herself into.

CHAPTER 27

Do not even *think* about missing tomorrow's blog post! Agh! I'm so excited I just may give away the surprise right here, right now on this live feed if I don't sign off fast. Just trust me on this one!

I'm soooo excited!

I'll post again here and share a link when the new post goes up. Just, please, please read it! Have I mentioned just how excited I am?

CHAPTER 28

Today I'm drinking my coffee from the simple brown ceramic mug that Miss Pauline just brought to my table. Soon you'll see why I'm here instead of in my sunroom at the end of the old gravel road. But first, go grab your coffee or tea, and I'll meet you right back here. Don't worry if it takes a few extra minutes to brew. I'll wait...right here at my table at the Sweet Tea and Sunshine Café in downtown Dodgeville.

Miss Pauline is getting a makeover!

Well, not Miss Pauline—her café! But her café is getting a makeover—for free!

Oh my heart, I was going to throw out little hints and fun facts throughout my entire post and surprise you all with this news at the end of today's post, but the minute I sat at this table, I just had to blurt it out! I'm tickled pink for Miss P!

Yesterday Henry and I were able to meet with a well-known designer from one of Greenville's best design firms. We met her here, at Miss Pauline's, and by the time we were ready to top off our meal with some of the café's famous peach cobbler, Molly, the designer, was giving Miss Pauline's a free makeover. This was all in conjunction with a contest the firm had run a few months back during one of the festivals in Greenville.

When Molly heard about Miss Pauline, she—like the rest of us—fell in love with her instantly. I mean, seriously, what's not to love about one of the dearest people in Dodgeville?

Did you know that Miss Pauline used to be my babysitter? When I lived here as a child, I didn't have any grandparents nearby. In fact, after my grandfather's passing, my paternal grandmother lived with my aunt and uncle out on the West Coast, and my grandparents on my mom's side were up in Minnesota. Though she was actually a few years younger than my parents, Miss Pauline had grayed prematurely (like my Henry), and my little six-year-old mind thought she was very old. I walked up to her after church one Sunday and said, "Will you be my grandma?"

Though she had never married to that point—and still never has—she was more than happy to serve as my "local grandmother," and she treated me just *as though that were actually her role. We had tea parties at her dining room table, which at that time I thought was positively luxurious. It was surrounded by six chairs with pink velvet chair cushions, each hand-embroidered with a deep-burgundy long-stemmed rose and three forest-green leaves. We drank from a gold-trimmed tea set that her childhood Sunday school teacher had left for her in her will.*

On my tenth birthday, before my family moved away from Dodgeville, Miss Pauline gave my mother that tea set, stipulating that when I was old enough to properly care for it, it was to become mine. It's on the shelf in our dining room and is the set I use when I write about having tea with Maggie and Kayla, our twin grandgirls. I've had Miss Pauline over for tea several times since moving back to the area, and we pick up right where we left off: she, loving on me; me, idolizing her every move.

When the local teenagers needed jobs in order to start saving for college, she'd hire them, pay them well, and promise them a bonus check on the day they graduated from college.

When new babies arrive, she gifts the parents with booties, a cap, and a matching blanket that she crochets specifically for their little one.

And recently, when she finally had saved up enough money for a "spiffy renovation of this old place," she announced through signs in the café and notices in the local newspaper that her restaurant would be closed for a month for renovation. However, that was just before a fire destroyed the house her elderly Aunt Adeline had lived in since birth—over eighty years. Miss Pauline took her savings and saw to it that her aunt had a nice place in the senior living center over in Glenbrook.

"My place can wait. It's not fancy, but it's safe, and it's clean. That's more than Aunt Adeline has at the moment, and I wouldn't feel right doing anything different."

So when the opportunity came for Molly to offer the free makeover from the contest to the well-deserving Miss Pauline, she jumped at the chance to do something nice for the woman so clearly and dearly loved by the citizens of her little town.

For the next month, Molly's firm will be working with the staff and a few of the regular customers of the Sweet Tea and Sunshine Café to design just the right style and décor. I'll keep you updated!

I know how much y'all love our sweet Miss P, and for this, I thank you...from my table in the corner...at Miss Pauline's Café...right on the square in Dodgeville.

CHAPTER 29

"Is it comfortable, or do you want it to recline a little more?" Allen's gift of the recumbent bike for Dad to use needed only a few adjustments so that Dad not only could lower himself onto the seat easily, but he could also safely and comfortably pedal while watching the evening news.

"Actually, sit it up just a little straighter. Yes…riiiight…there!" Dad began pedaling in place with the ease and zeal of a child sitting on a tricycle, riding in circles around the driveway. This would be a game-changing addition to Dad's exercise routine.

"Now remember your promise: thirty minutes a day—even though they don't all have to be done in one sitting. We may be headed back to Iowa tomorrow, but I'm going to check in on you, and I want to hear that you've been riding!"

Allen was good for Dad. He could encourage him and instruct him with precision, all while letting him know that he was honored and respected, even in the midst of so many physical changes. His visits were bright spots for Mom and Dad—and for us. Henry's boys had great admiration for this metropolitan businessman turned rural-Iowa nurse and had called him "Uncle Allen" from the get-go.

"Hey, I have an idea!"

"Now you sound like your sister!" Dad looked across the room at me and smirked at Allen's having used my all-too-familiar phrase.

"Let's have the artistic Henry draw you a map from here to our house in Iowa. The goal will be to pedal a little bit each day, each session getting you a little closer to Iowa." He looked directly at Henry as he spoke the rest. "It may be a good idea to mark some of Dad's favorite regular 'stopping points' along the way to our house. That way it won't feel so overwhelming to start pedaling all the way out to Iowa." He turned back to Dad. "Are you up for the challenge?"

"I'll do it. When Dr. Michaels said my faithful exercise was helping to keep the Parkinson's in check, that was enough motivation for me. If making these pedals move while I sit and read or watch the news keeps me mobile, you'd better believe I'll do it! Besides, I wouldn't want my two favorite nurses upset with me."

CHAPTER 30

Today I'm drinking my coffee from a bright yellow mug that simply says, "Family." Soon you'll see why. But first, go grab your coffee or tea, and I'll meet you right back here. Don't worry if it takes a few extra minutes to brew. I'll wait...right here at the end of the old gravel road.

My brother, Allen, and his precious wife, Lydia, had lived the big-city life for the first twenty-three years of their marriage. They worked long, hard hours, felt stressed more often than not, and knew that in spite of Allen's years of education and experience in the field of international law and Lydia's in corporate finance, they both needed a major change. Continuing to do what they were doing was going to bring the same results.

At the age of forty-six (they share a November birthday), they donned their collegiate-style backpacks and headed back to college, hoping to fast-track it through nursing school so that they could devote their lives to helping others. Yes, they were blessed to have had high-level jobs that paid well, now allowing them to focus on their education without having to worry about the financial aspects that generally come with higher education. But they also had brilliant minds, determination, and a motivation to make a major life change.

When these two go-getters make a plan, they follow it through—in big fashion.

Three years into their studies, Lydia's grandfather passed away, and it prodded her to look into a specialty in gerontological nursing. She felt compelled to further her studies and devote her skills to helping the elderly.

The day after Allen and Lydia graduated with their BSN degrees from the University of Wisconsin, they loaded their now minimal belongings into a rental moving truck and headed over to Minneapolis. The following Wednesday, Allen began his work at a local hospital, and Lydia began classes at the University of Minnesota to become a gerontological nurse practitioner.

After completing her degree two years ago, she and Allen both accepted positions just outside of Des Moines, Iowa. We are all so extremely proud of them. And they couldn't be happier, doing what they love.

Suffice it to say, Mom and Dad think Lydia hung the moon. She has been— and continues to be—a huge blessing to all of us, especially since Dad's Parkinson's diagnosis. I confess, it's nice to have some smart medical folks in the family.

Your kind notes, encouraging words, and private messages, all filled with love for my entire family, have meant the world to Henry and me, and for this, I thank you...from my desk in the sunroom...at the back of the house...at the end of the old gravel road.

CHAPTER 31

My brother and sister-in-law were here for a visit recently, and even though I wrote about it on the blog this morning, I just had to do a quick live feed to give a shout out to the beauty of all that is *family*.

Listening. Caring. Arguing. Learning. Encouraging. Hurting. Fighting. Forgiving. Helping. Sharing. Working together. Respecting.

Loving.

I know that not everyone watching this live feed will agree. You might have had an extremely difficult upbringing, or you might even be in a sad family situation at this moment. Though I cannot fully relate to that with a firsthand-knowledge kind of understanding, I can care, and I can encourage you to overcome and to create *family* wherever you are.

CHAPTER 32

"I just heard from Scheduling, and I was able to get my flights lined up around Dodgeville Days. My last trip that week will be a one-day trip on Tuesday, but I'll be back that night, so I can help you with any last-minute prep for the boys' visits and any setup downtown we need to do later that week. I don't fly out again until the following Thursday, so I can volunteer with you that next week in Mrs. Markham's class. Have you heard yet as to when everyone's getting in?"

"Ben's group will be here Thursday night; Jonathan will be here by noon on Friday. I love that schedule, by the way! How'd you get out of the Rome trip that week?"

"Andrew took it. Remember my telling you about him?"

I nodded in reply, my mouth already busy with chewing an almond I had popped into my mouth instead of into the salad with the others.

"We need to have lunch with him one of these times when you're up in Charlotte with me. He's one sharp guy, and I've loved having him in the right seat with me a few times. He just did his check ride last month and got promoted to captain, so we won't fly together as much now—if at all. But, yeah, he took the trip to Rome for me. They gave me one to London later next month, so that will take care of fulfilling my hours."

"Thanks for getting that in early. It puts my mind at ease, knowing you'll be around. Besides, I *always* like it when you're around." Kissing across the kitchen counter was one of our favorite meal-prep routines, and now seemed like as good a time as any!

"Oh, Wilbur, there's no need to be jealous. We love you, too." Henry reached down to scratch behind Wilbur's left ear as he jumped up to rest his paw on Henry's arm as if to say, "Hey, don't forget about me!"

"I liked your idea of reusing some of the older blog posts during the week leading up to Dodgeville Days. That gives me time to volunteer, prepare for the family, and help Molly with any finishing touches over at Sweet Tea and Sunshine."

"Planning to pick some random ones, or are you going to run an old series?"

"Italian or Bleu Cheese?"

"Bleu Cheese tonight."

From the very start, close to ten years ago now, Henry had worked right alongside me in the kitchen. Tonight was no different. Our nearly choreographed routine kept us seamlessly weaving in and out—in both our steps and our conversation.

"I thought I'd post the four-parter about our love story. We've had so many new followers over the last few years that I feel like I want to share that again." I set the bottle of dressing near his plate at the table and then turned to look at him. "What are your thoughts on that?"

"It sounds perfect. I was hoping you'd share that again sometime. I agree. It's time. Besides, it's a pretty rippin'-good love story, if you ask me." He headed over to give me another quick kiss, only to be cut short by Wilbur's desire to get there first.

CHAPTER 33

Today I'm drinking my coffee from a mug my sister-in-law gave me when she was here. In fact, she gave me a matching oven mitt and apron that say the same thing as the mug. On a charcoal-gray background, the following words, along with a silhouette of a rolling pin, appear in white: Creating Meals and Memories. *They are adorable and extra special because she made them for me. This was the perfect mug for today, because I'm planning to spend some time on creating freezer meals in a little bit. But first, go grab your coffee or tea, and I'll meet you back here. Don't worry if it takes a few extra minutes to brew. I'll wait...right here at the end of the old gravel road.*

I'll tell you right now that these next four real-life stories are being pre-posted and scheduled to go live on future days. We're headed into the biggest event of the year in our sweet little town, Dodgeville Days, and not only is our family coming to town for the festival, but we are having a booth again this year for The Old Gravel Road. *We love meeting the visitors to town, and we've contracted with Miss Pauline to carry some of her cute Dodgeville mugs in addition to some of the merchandise we have available on our website: T-shirts, caps, aprons, tote bags, and wall art.*

Speaking of dear Miss P, Decorator Molly told me just this morning that the makeover and renovations to the Sweet Tea and Sunshine Café are nearly complete. My lips are sealed until the official reveal, but suffice it to say, it's nothing short of amazing! Miss P is planning a "Grand Reopening" during Dodgeville Days. So consider this your official invitation to stop by our happy little town the last weekend in March— just be sure to save room for some of the best macaroni and cheese you've ever eaten, available daily at the Sweet Tea and Sunshine Café on the square. Oh, and while you're there, pick up a few of her fresh strawberry fry pies—the berries come straight from outside Columbia, and they're supposed to be huge this year. You can thank me later!

I'll be back "live" before the festival, but until then, Henry and I hope that you'll enjoy reading our love story via a series of posts that we shared early in the history of our blog. You have welcomed us into your homes and hearts through this website, and for this, we are thankful...from our house at the end of the old gravel road.

And now, the first installment of our love story...and, ah, what a sweet, sweet love story it is...!

My dear Henry got his pilot's license before he got his driver's license. For as long as he can remember, Henry has loved all things related to aviation. In fact, he is more passionate about flying than nearly anyone else I know is about their job. He eats, breathes, and sleeps flying.

My dear Henry graduated from college with a bachelor of science degree in math education, fulfilling his parents' desire that he get a degree that he could "fall back on if this whole flying thing doesn't pan out." Four months after graduation, he signed on with a major airline and has flown ever since for each of the airlines affiliated with that company.

My dear Henry is a caring, kind, hardworking, and generous man. He is a wonderful father, grandfather, and friend.

But my dear Henry was not always my dear Henry.

Following his first full year of work with the airlines, Henry met Liz Richardson, a kindergarten teacher who was originally from Estes Park, Colorado. Liz had moved to that area three years before that and had rented a small, one-bedroom apartment above the garage of the house that was next door to the fire station. It was noisy, but the rent was cheap, and Liz was still paying off her college loans.

During that time period, my mom volunteered in the elementary school library every Wednesday afternoon. She thrived on helping the kindergarten students find age-appropriate books that they could check out to take home for the next week. As a classically trained musician, she had a tender spot in her heart for the arts and found the colorful pictures and drawings stimulating to the students' developing young minds. She often said that those pictures could teach an early elementary child as much as the word pictures painted within the pages of the chapter books that the older children were able to read.

Mom felt that volunteering in our schools not only gave her the opportunity to hear what was going on within the school; it also gave her the right to be heard when she gave input from a parent's point of view. Even in those few hours in the school library each week, she made a difference.

It's also where she met Miss Liz Richardson. Liz was dating a young pilot, and as soon as she heard Mom tell one of the students that her husband flew big airplanes, she asked if they could meet for coffee at the mall after school sometime. She needed input from someone who understood what it was like to date—and marry?—a pilot who would be traveling often, sometimes outside the country. She hadn't wanted things to get too serious with Henry Evans if she wasn't up for the challenge over the long haul.

Dad was actually doing several domestic flights each week during that year, so when he got home from a trip out West, Mom told him all about this nice teacher and her young-pilot boyfriend. Dad was impressed with what he was hearing about the character of the young pilot and mentioned that it may be fun to have the couple over for dinner sometime when Henry was visiting, primarily so that the two men could "talk flying."

I remember asking if I could be excused from the table early that night. I was fifteen, and talking on the phone about boys with my friends far outranked listening to more talk about airplanes. Besides, even though I really didn't know Miss Richardson, and even though she taught in the elementary school, and I was in the high school, talking to a teacher outside of the classroom just wasn't all that fun.

Again, I was fifteen. A very, very self-focused fifteen.

Miss Richardson and the pilot guy got married in the large, scenic backyard of her parents' home in Colorado. We saw their photo album when they came over for dessert and coffee one evening after they got back from their honeymoon. I remember a little about the pictures, but little about the evening or the people. We *were about to move again, which, to me, meant I needed to spend every moment I possibly could talking with my friends, so I asked to be excused after only a few glances at the album. The Evanses were nice, but they were my parents' friends, not mine, though we all definitely considered them "family friends."*

Think you know where this is going? You may know the ultimate ending already—at least a little bit of it—but there were so many surprises along the way (even for all of us) that I can't wait to share them—in the next post—from my desk in the sunroom...at the back of the house...at the end of the old gravel road.

CHAPTER 34

"I'd like to have the house completely ready by Monday night of Dodgeville Days week, before you leave on Tuesday, so would you have about forty-five minutes to an hour today to help me move the couch out of the nook in the bonus room, vacuum up there, and pull out the air mattresses for the girls? I know it's still a couple of weeks out, but I'd like to get a jump start on things! Oh, and...no, I think that's it for now."

"Sure. Let me take Wilbur out before we get started on everything."

"You're awesome—and cute! Thanks, honey. Katy Liddle and I are going berry picking at the you-pick farm outside of Columbia on Tuesday. It's the one thing Miss Pauline would let us do to help her in the kitchen before Dodgeville Days. She's making a boatload of her little "fry pies" on Thursday, so Tuesday is the perfect day for us to go pickin'. I'll try to grab an extra bucket for us to have so that we'll have plenty on hand when the family's here. When I called to make sure the berries would be ready, the owner said that this was a great year for them—they're a little earlier than normal, and they're apparently already huge. Okay, give me about five minutes, and I'll have the budget spreadsheet opened and ready to go. Then we can head upstairs."

Our weekly "family budget meetings" over coffee together in the sunroom were sometimes tedious—but always helpful for keeping us on track. With Henry's mandatory retirement age inching nearer, we had tweaked our existing budget to accommodate putting more into savings and less into accumulating more *stuff*. Looking at the real numbers—together—kept us aware of where the money *had been* spent, *needed* to be spent, and still *could be* spent, and we both found it very freeing not to have to think about it the rest of the week, knowing that we were keeping our spending in line with our long-term priorities.

"All right, here we go: Anderson and Sons Hardware, on the twelfth..." Henry paused, allowing me time to type the *when* and *where* into their designated columns on the spreadsheet, "$18.32. That was for the boards you wanted for the extra sign for the booth. Okay, next: Hendricksens' G and G, also on the twelfth...."

CHAPTER 35

We're giving away a "Dodgeville Bundle" next week during Dodgeville Days. So why am I jumping on here to tell *you* about it? Because Henry wants to give our blog followers a chance to win a bundle even if they can't be here in South Carolina for the festival. Yep! We're giving away a second bundle—only available to our followers.

Here's what's included:
* 1 "I heart Dodgeville" mug (the mug is brown and black)
* 1 mug, mitt, and apron set in black: "Creating Meals and Memories" (my sister-in-law is donating a set, isn't that sweet?)
* 1 "new town motto" tote bag (black)
* 1 8x10 canvas wall art: "Life is more exciting when you take the gravel road."

So how can you enter? I'm glad you asked! Click on the "go to the website" option at the end of this feed to go directly to the entry form on our website. You can also go straight to the website, click on the "Dodgeville Days Giveaway" box on the home page, fill in the form, and click "Submit." The rules and terms are clearly spelled out there, so be sure to read those first. Our third-party service will randomly select one winner from those who 1) entered the giveaway and 2) are also subscribed to follow our blog. So be sure to subscribe if you haven't already done so!

Good luck on the giveaway! For those of you who are able to attend Dodgeville Days in person, be sure to stop by our booth, enter to win the "Locals-Only Bundle," and exchange howdies with us! We can't wait to see y'all down on the square!

CHAPTER 36

Pilots pretty much have the ability to live wherever they choose and "commute" to their home base airport for work. Allen and I used to get a kick out of telling people that our dad worked several hours away in another state, and that he commuted to work! It's unusual for the general population to think of commuting that way, but for those in the airline industry, it's quite common.

(This is probably a good time to tell you that this is part two in a four-part series. Now's a good time to stop and read my last post if you haven't read it yet!)

Henry and Liz chose to live in Connecticut, making his home base of Boston fairly easy to access. We annually exchanged Christmas cards, and even took them out for dinner when we were in Connecticut over spring break during my senior year of high school. My parents had gifted me a trip to tour the New England states as part of my high school graduation gift.

The Evanses hadn't changed much, other than the fact that Liz was just about seven months pregnant with their first child. After dinner, they invited all of us over to their house for a quick peek at the nursery they had just painted, and it was fun to see their excitement over entering this next season of life. I remember thinking how cute they were in their love for each other and hoping that my husband and I would be that happy someday—that is, after I graduated from high school, college, and, well, actually had a husband!

When I expressed those thoughts to Mom on the trip back to the hotel that night, she smiled and said, "You've got plenty of time to think about such things, dear one. Don't be in a hurry."

Our family was excited when the announcement arrived, telling us that the Evanses' first son, Jonathan, had been born. He was born the day I graduated from high school.

Two years later, we received another announcement, this time telling us of Benjamin's birth. I was headed into my junior year of college.

Between my junior and senior years of college, I worked as a camp counselor just outside of Boston. Our parents strongly encouraged both Allen and me to spend one summer using our talents, skills, and abilities to give back to others in our community or within a charitable organization. Though my interest and skills were being honed through my double major of music and English education, I knew that working with kids that summer would grow me as a person and would help me see outside my own comfortable world.

Suffice it to say, I learned more from my campers than they learned from me. I also learned more about Liz Evans that summer. Henry was moving up the ranks with the airlines, and his current schedule had him flying out to California on Fridays, returning to their home in Connecticut late Saturday evening. Liz invited me to spend all or part of my weekends at "a real house." I had fun playing with the boys and giving Liz a little break in the afternoon before helping with supper and then heading back to camp. She would get the boys settled into bed, and soon thereafter, Henry would get home, ready to hit the sack as well.

Liz and I talked about everything on those short visits. For me, it was nice to have a place to escape to after the rugged accommodations of camp life. Liz enjoyed the adult company while Henry was away. We talked about all things education. The rest of the conversation usually led to dating, marriage, children, and life in general.

At the time, I was in a long-distance relationship that was waning. My boyfriend, Kip, had graduated the year before and was already working as a high school science teacher in Virginia. We seemed to be drifting apart, but I felt like I needed to try harder to love him since he was such a great guy. In one of our first conversations that summer, Liz wisely told me, "Two great people don't necessarily make one great couple. If it doesn't work out, it doesn't mean that anything was wrong. It may simply mean that it just wasn't right."

By the end of the summer, Kip and I acknowledged that "it just wasn't right," and we remain friends to this day. (By the way, he still lives in Virginia—with his wife and five children—and we annually exchange Christmas cards. I got his permission to share his part in my story with you.)

Sweet Liz mentioned often how tired she was that summer. I figured that with a newborn and a toddler, it was only natural for her to tire easily. It wasn't until Jonathan was in kindergarten that we found out her weariness over the past three years had been trying to tell her something.

CHAPTER 37

"No way, Molly. We can't accept that. Your crew is so busy already. Seriously. The grand reopening for Sweet Tea and Sunshine is in two weeks! You're a sweetheart, but we could *not* do that to you."

Before I could ask for an update on Miss P's Café—out of true curiosity as well as in an attempt to change the subject—Molly began listing off the points on the timeline for "Operation Bonus Room."

"By tomorrow afternoon at two o'clock, you need to clear *everything* out of the craft nook in the bonus room. I'm meeting Ellie and her team here. We'll talk over the master plan in the actual room, and the painters will be here next Wednesday. It won't take them long at all. They've got it down to a science. It really is spectacular the way they seamlessly choreograph the process from start to finish. They'll do the second coat on Thursday morning—and trust me on this, they are early risers, so they'll probably want to get started by seven. At nine that morning, the...."

"Wait!"

She paused, appeared shocked by my one-syllable, loudly spoken request, and said, "Yessssss, Bitsy?"

"How did you know that I have a craft nook in the bonus room? When you came to the house, we only went as far as the kitchen and sunroom. How do you know these things?"

"Henry's been in on it for a few days now. In fact, knowing you had a committee meeting last Thursday for the Dodgeville Days closing ceremony, he invited Ellie and me over for a walkthrough. We got so much accomplished! He was a huge help to us, so please don't be upset with him!"

"Are you kidding me? How could I be upset with him when he's been so good at keeping the secret? Oh, and one other question: Who is Ellie?"

"Silly me. I introduced her to Henry, of course, but I forgot that you haven't met her yet. Ellie is my younger sister. She's been my apprentice this past year, and we've given her a team of her own at the firm. We think so much alike that our work is completely interchangeable. Now back to that schedule."

The rest of the conversation, as its beginning, is still a whirl of words in my mind: *makeover, bonus room, paint, bed, reading nook*, and the biggie— *four days.*

Four days. How? Why? Wow! And then...tears, the kind that find their source in that feeling of overwhelming gratitude.

Molly, effervescent but ever professional Molly, drew the conversation to a close by confirming my e-mail address and telling me that the plans needed my okay by four thirty that afternoon. Henry had consented to them already, but she had, at his suggestion, tweaked a few things that were more elaborate than our intent for the use of the room, and she wanted me to be aware of them—and give my approval or suggest any minor changes.

CHAPTER 38

"I love this, Henry! What a great idea! How did you come up with that?"

"Your idea board was all I needed. I snuck online while you were writing last week. I merely pieced the three most important elements together and left the rest to Molly and her team. Well, actually, did Molly tell you about her sister?"

"Yes. Ellie? I'm sure she'll be just as amazing as Molly or Molly wouldn't have her take on the project. But start at the beginning and tell me *everything* she told you when she called that day. Don't leave *anything* out! No detours, Captain!"

Henry spent the next twenty minutes rehearsing the conversation he had with Molly. She had asked him to keep it a secret, and he had won a gold star in that department!

When Henry and I made the decision to gift (confidentially) our free makeover (and a little more) to Miss Pauline in gratitude for her sacrificial giving to others and to our community, Molly had been quite overwhelmed by that act. Additionally, the people of Dodgeville were so impressed with Molly's willingness to come to our little town and give their favorite café a new look that two other businesses had already contacted her firm to do some work on "upgrading" their stores as well. That had sealed it in her mind—she now wanted to do something special for us to show her gratitude.

Since Miss Pauline was never to know that we had forgone our free makeover, Molly had only two people she *could* contact: Henry or my mom. She knew, based on something I had told her in the initial interview, that my mom and I talk several times a week. I think she was afraid my mom may "let me in on a little secret," so she reached out to Henry, got access to the one room he knew I wanted to make some changes to—the bonus room over the garage—and drew up a plan:

* The craft nook will now be moved to the other side of the room, where a built-in desk and storage area will be created to house my supplies.
* The now-empty craft nook will become the home of a "window seat/daybed." Because of our initial desire to have bunk beds there (which Molly said would make the area unfunctional the rest of the time), she designed a pull-out "drawer" under the window seat/daybed that will contain a trundle bed. How awesome is that?
* The remaining space in the old craft nook will now have bookshelves and lighting so that the window-seat element of it can serve as a "reading nook" during the times when the beds aren't being used.
* The entire bonus room will be painted to give

it a fresh look and brighten things up a bit. The game and seating areas will remain the same since we bought the couch for up there as our Christmas gift to ourselves only a few months ago.

And they are able to do all of this in four or five days!

"Henry, please don't wake me up from this dream. Please!" The gentle hug that followed said that he understood the source of the tears that began to flow down my cheeks.

In my usual cry-it-out, dry-it-up, and-then-keep-moving-forward way, I suddenly stepped back from his hug, looked him in the eyes, and said, "We'd better get busy clearing out that craft nook. I don't want to delay their work by even one minute!" And with that, we both headed up the stairway, Wilbur and his happily wagging tail close behind.

CHAPTER 39

Y'all need to know...that *I* know...that y'all probably *don't* know...that I know...just *how* blessed I am to have people from all over the globe caring about our little town down here in South Carolina.

Sharing their stories, including you in the ups and downs of the residents of Dodgeville, and welcoming you into the community that we call home is what makes my heart sing, even when it's overcome with...well, life.

So *thank* you. In fact, Henry and I *both* thank you.

It may sound hokey to those who have only recently added themselves into *The Old Gravel Road* sites by following, subscribing, or in some form catching tidbits of our stories, but we consider you part of our extended, though online, family. You matter to us, and it's why we love when you connect with us via e-mail, private messages, comments, and whatever other ways we've heard from you.

You. Matter. To. Us.

Are you following along on the blog right now? I'm sharing four posts I wrote a few years ago. It's Henry's and my love story. Aww...! Seriously, though, you'll learn a lot about us if you take a minute to follow those, so consider this your personal invitation to do so.

Our family is coming for a visit in the near future, we have a minor—but very major—makeover happening in the bonus room above our garage this week, and the annual big celebration of our little town takes place soon. So, yep, we're a little preoccupied these days.

However, I just had to pop on here and let you know that you matter! I also felt compelled to say a huge thank you for giving us the privilege of including you in our lives, because you have so graciously included us in yours.

Our house at the end of the old gravel road is about to get really noisy—the crew is about to arrive to finish the trundle-bed window seat....

Oops, I was going to save that surprise for the blog next week, so don't tell anyone, okay?

And on that blunder, I'll head out for the day. See you soon!

(But seriously, I can hardly wait to tell y'all this story and show you this room. Oh. My. Heart!)

CHAPTER 40

Two days before Jonathan's Christmas break from kindergarten, Liz collapsed in the kitchen of their Connecticut home. Henry was out on a short one-day trip, and he actually landed about twenty minutes early—which proved to be a blessing on many counts.

As was his custom, Henry called Liz before leaving the airport. Unable to reach her, he naturally assumed that she was putting the boys to bed and had turned down the volume on the phone's ringer in order to avoid waking them. He knew she'd been a little extra tired lately, and he decided to pick up some flowers at the local grocer's on his way into town. Unfortunately, traffic was quite heavy, so the flowers could wait; he'd head straight home.

Their next-door neighbors in the cul-de-sac, who Liz often said reminded them of Ed and Lori Hall (my parents), were there in a heartbeat when Henry called and said he'd found Liz on the kitchen floor. He had already called for an ambulance, but he needed someone to stay with the boys. He didn't know how long she had been there, but he knew he'd never been so happy for heavy traffic that had prohibited him from making additional stops on the way home.

Her breast cancer had been present long enough that her body could no longer mask the symptoms or keep her activity level at the rate she had been going. The diagnosis was quick to arrive and certain enough to cause Liz's parents to catch the first flight to Connecticut— with the plan to begin looking for a home in the area. Finding a home for sale in New England during the winter months was unlikely to be easy, but with Henry's travel, they all felt it may be the best solution.

Over the course of the next seven years, Liz fought hard. She underwent surgeries, treatment programs, and all the tender love and care that Henry, her parents, her friends, and her community could bestow on her. I wrote to her every now and then, keeping in touch about my comings and goings as a journalist in the Midwest.

Liz encouraged me often during those difficult years as a single woman whose friends were not only getting married but who were now parents, some with multiple children already. I tried to cheer her with funny anecdotal stories I had covered for the newspaper. I called a few times when Mom told me that it may not be long, but she was weak, and it was tiring for her to talk on the phone. When her letters arrived, however, they were full of life and the kind of advice she had given me on those weekend trips to see her the summer I had worked as a camp counselor.

I still have a few of them.

In the spring of that seventh year, Liz's body succumbed to the disease that now left Henry a widower at the age of forty.

Jonathan was twelve; Benjamin was ten.

I was thirty, still single, and fully devoted to establishing my career as a local reporter for a growing newspaper in the Midwest.

CHAPTER 41

"Don't apologize. I love your old-school scheduling methods. That giant chalkboard calendar has been the brains of this family for nearly ten years."

"Hey, wait a minute. The *chalkboard* is the brains of this family?" I mostly threw his comment back to him because I loved to see my calm, smart, quick-thinking husband get flustered as he tried to dig his way out of a verbal blunder. A little bit cruel, but a whole lotta fun!

"No, what I meant was…. Wait. You're doing that thing again, aren't you?"

With nothing more than a smirk from both of us doubling as an understood reply, we both chuckled and once again focused our attention on the large calendar that had proudly retained its prominent position on the kitchen wall since the week after we had moved into the house nine years ago. At the end of each month I took a photo of the calendar, showing what we had done and what we should plan for/schedule the following year. It wasn't the cool digital style used by many of our younger friends and family members, but it was the approved, proven, and preferred method for the Evans household.

I grabbed a piece of chalk and wrote the following list as I spoke. I found myself saying the words slowly enough that my writing and speaking of the one- or two-word event titles ended in perfect unison.

> "Tuesday: I **volunteer** at school in the morning; you fly to **Pittsburgh** and back
>
> Wednesday: Ellie's **paint crew** arrives at **7:15**; we **assemble the booth** in the garage
>
> Thursday: Ellie's **crews** arrive at **7:15**; we shop in **Greenville**"

Henry interrupted the list making with an additional plan: "How about if we go on a date to our favorite little restaurant while we're in Greenville? The service is pretty quick there, and we'll need to eat anyhow. We can hit all the non-grocery stores in the morning, grab some lunch, and then finish with the warehouse store on the way back out of town. Does that plan work, Mrs. Evans?"

"It's perfect, Mr. Evans. And sweet of you to think of it." *Ahh, there's that handsome sideways smirkish smile.*

> "Friday: **Ellie** and her team arrive at 7:15 to complete the build for the bed and bookshelves and begin the decorating aspect; you fly to **Philly** and back; I make **freezer**

meals to have when the family is here

Saturday: **Laundry**; I have a Dodgeville Days (**DD**) meeting at 10:00; you are going to help Sherriff Lehman post **parking signs** around town

Sunday: **Church** and **dinner** with Mom and Dad

Monday: Ellie's crew finishes the **bonus room**—and we're not allowed up there until **2:00**

Tuesday: You fly to **Boston** and back; Katy and I pick **strawberries** near Columbia for Miss P's fry pies

Wednesday: We take the morning off! And then...we help Decorator Molly with any last-minute **décor** at the Sweet Tea and Sunshine Café; we're invited to a private grand-reopening **reception** at Miss P's at 4:00; I also want to do a final **cleaning** for the family's visit.

Thursday: I help Miss P and Katy make **fry pies**; you and Dad are going **fishing** in the morning so that Mom can help us over at Miss P's— Would you want to just plan to take him to lunch that day, too? It might be best for everyone if we didn't have to worry about stopping to prepare lunches. **Ben and Izzy** will be here around

4:00, so if there's anything we need done, let's have it done before they arrive. Once those darlin' little twins arrive, I don't want to be distracted by tedium! A little before **7:00**, I need to help **Pastor Dave** with a few things for the official opening ceremony; and believe it or not, that's it for Friday—other than enjoying the time with family and checking in on the booth now and then.

Friday: In the morning we need to work at the **booth**—Ben said he'd help with that; **Jonathan** will be here around **11:00**, so Izzy and the girls will be here to help him get unloaded, and they'll meet us downtown at noon. The rest of Friday we just get to enjoy the festival! I've got people lined up for the booth the rest of the time—other than a few time slots that we're going to be there.

Saturday: Our only *official* events are to serve at the chicken and waffles **breakfast** at GlenVille High and cover the **booth** from **12:00** to **1:30**. Oh, and I'm supposed to be available to help Pastor Dave at **6:15** at the **closing ceremony**. We can just load the booth into the truck after that, and Izzy can help me with any merchandise that's left.

Did I leave *anything* out?"

"Actually, I was about to ask if there was anything left in town that you *hadn't* scheduled on the chalkboard!" His teasing belied the fact that he loved that we were active in the community—and that he loved Dodgeville and its residents as much as I did.

"I know it sounds like a lot, but there really is a lot of down time to just enjoy every minute with the boys."

We had long called Henry's sons "the boys," and the term, though unchanged, had now come to include Ben's wife, Izzy, and their twins, Maggie and Kayla.

CHAPTER 42

I should probably add at the beginning of this fourth and final post in the series that I was indeed a journalist at this time in Henry's and my love story. I had taught both English and music my first two years out of college. I was engaged to a well-liked teacher at the school, but he—unbeknownst to me—was also interested in a wealthy heiress who lived outside of Atlanta. That's not a blog post I care to write, so I'll simply state that as a woman of faith I can share that I now think God greatly protected me from my own naivete regarding that relationship. It was a hurtful ending with deep scars that, over time, turned into a garden where compassion and empathy took root in my heart.

When our relationship ended, I cancelled my contract for the following year, not knowing where I was headed next. I only knew that I didn't want to be "poor Miss Hall," as I felt I had been labeled at the school. My parents had just moved back to Dodgeville after many years away, so I applied for a position at what was then Dodgeville High School, thinking that it would be nice to be near family. However, there were no positions available until the second half of the school year.

Since this is a post about our love story, I'll get to the bottom line of this rabbit trail and tell you that my brother Allen had a connection with the editor of a fledgling newspaper in Virginia who hired me to proofread and edit other writers' pieces. After two years of editing, I increasingly found myself longing to be the one writing the articles. I drafted a sample article, an outline of my goals for the column, and all but begged the senior editor for a break into writing. I'll never know what he saw in that hokey little article, but he gave me an opportunity to write, and the column took off faster and with a wider readership than any of us could have hoped for. The rest, as they say, is history.

It's also one of the ways in which Henry and I reconnected on a more personal level several years following Liz's death.

Henry read my column while in a hotel lobby near Richmond. He sent a note in care of the newspaper, telling me how much he had enjoyed the article and how he was thrilled to see that I was doing so *well. It was bland, polite, kind, and clearly written* from *an old family friend* to *an old family friend.*

When I told my parents about the kind note of encouragement I had received from their buddy Henry Evans, Dad—surprisingly, not Mom—began thinking about possibilities that were on neither Henry's nor my radar!

To this day, my father denies that he had anything to do with the fact that a mere six weeks after I received the note from Henry, he and Henry were scheduled to fly as captain and copilot of the same flight to London. Dad, dear sweet Dad, used every mile to extol my praises to poor Henry.

On the return flight, Henry shared with Dad that he was realizing how lonely he was and how his boys were at the point that they were ready to have a more constant female influence in their lives. His parents lived overseas, and they were loving and helpful—as were Liz's parents—but it wasn't the same.

Henry was ready to love again, and for the first time since Liz's passing, he was able to voice those longings—to my dad.

My sweet father ended the flight with these words, "Now Henry, I'm not trying to push my Bitsy on you, but it sounds like you're ready to start dating again. So why not start with the best. You've had the best already, so don't just settle for 'second best.' Choose the one who is best for you—and for your boys—in this unique season of your life."

I was mortified—and dare I confess, secretly thrilled—when I learned that Dad gave Henry one of his business cards...with my phone number on the back! "Keep in touch, Henry!"

On our first dinner date, Henry knew. I wasn't in that zone yet. My guarded heart needed more time. I also needed to spend some time with the boys, who were both in college and who were more than aware that the father they loved had not only loved their mother dearly but also needed someone to love in the present. They were on board from the start.

A mere eight months later, with the biggest grin I've ever seen on his face, my father walked me down the central path toward the gazebo behind the Dodgeville Community Church, where

Pastor Dave officiated the ceremony that united Beulah Lee Hall and Henry James Evans.

Henry's boys, Jonathan and Benjamin, were our "men of honor." Jonathan stood to my left; Benjamin, on Henry's right. We had no other attendants. It was as we all wanted it, and it served as the cornerstone for the foundation of our new family unit.

The boys' grandparents were very much a part of their lives before Henry and I were married, and they remain so to this day. My parents have been added to that exclusive group, and the way in which Henry's parents and Liz's parents have included them has been nothing short of exemplary. Their acceptance of my parents—and of me—has made all the difference in how the boys have accepted me.

Early in our marriage, Henry held a "family meeting," reminding all of us that we had been given the gift of each other. He made it clear that we each should not only cherish our memories of Liz, but we should feel free to speak of those memories.

We all fondly remember Liz. We speak of her as the occasion presents itself, but we also acknowledge that love comes in varying forms, in varying ways, and that it deserves our greatest efforts, attention, and time—in this moment.

We are constantly growing, learning, changing, moving forward, and aware that we are blessed by the gifts we have in each other.

And for this...we are grateful.

So that's where it all began. It's also how I came to begin sharing our lives with you...from my desk in the sunroom...at the back of the house...at the end of the old gravel road.

CHAPTER 43

The fourth scheduled post about Henry's and my love story just went live on the blog. Since I subscribe to my own blog—don't judge; I do it to make sure the e-mails go out on time!—I just read through it when it arrived in my in-box. It still gives me goosebumps.

However, that's not why I'm here. I realized that I talked about what used to be Dodgeville High School, and it occurred to me that I don't think I've ever shared with you why there is no *longer* a Dodgeville High School.

I think it was about fifteen years ago—I'm not sure of the exact timing, but I know that it was before we moved here. Anyhow, it became clear that Dodgeville's small high school and Glenbrook's small high school should consolidate. The towns were basically "sisters" anyway, so joining forces would help to increase the quality of education they could provide and would also help to strengthen the impact of their sports, music, and drama departments.

It sounds fairly simple, right—since both schools already existed, had the necessary faculty and staff in place, and had a building in Glenbrook that had plenty of room for everyone? For the most part, it was.

The problem that nearly became the end of the entire project, however, should have been one of the easiest aspects of consolidation: What should they name the school?

As would be expected, the Dodgeville residents felt that it should be called Dodgeville High, and the Glenbrook residents felt it should be Glenbrook High, both towns clearly feeling that the other should accommodate its choice. After only a few back-and-forth exchanges in the first two meetings of the consolidated school board, it was determined that to maintain unity between the sister towns, a new name was necessary.

A new set of controversies sprang from that, because when Glenbrook offered a name of one of its outstanding citizens that the school could be named after, Dodgeville followed suit. Again, the process was forced to take another direction.

This went on for several months, with each town wanting to retain its rights to ownership of the school through the name that would be selected.

Apparently the brother-and-sister team on the new board (he, from Glenbrook; she, from Dodgeville) came up with the idea of combining the names of the two towns so that each would be properly represented. Problem solved.

Not so fast. We're not done with this yet.

Even though you may think that would take care of everything, it created a dig-your-heels-in battle that was even more controversial than the previous ones had been: Which town's name should come first?

Because I don't wish to share anything that would make you think evil of either of our little towns, let me jump to the ending.

It was decided, with a few reluctantly raised hands and accompanied by several hesitant "ayes," that Glenbrook should get first place in the name. This was due to the fact that the new school would be located just outside Glenbrook—nearer in proximity to Glenbrook than to Dodgeville.

The only stipulation was that the syllables that represented the names of the two towns should *each* be capitalized. Therefore, I am happy to share that we are now a joyfully unified school, called by the carefully chosen name of GlenVille High School, with a capital *G...and* a capital *V*.

CHAPTER 44

"I'm not even sure where to begin." My tears were held in check by the wonder of soaking it all in. "It's a bit overwhelming." I spoke to Ellie, but I was looking at Henry...and then at Ellie...and then at Molly...and then at the built-in craft unit...the window-seat daybed...the study/work area...and the color scheme that made me never want to leave the bonus room!

"How did you know exactly what I wanted when I didn't even know myself?"

"I listened. And I heard the heart behind your words."

"I told you she was good!" Molly's pride in her sister's work was evident as she graciously took the back seat for the praise on this one.

"Well thanks, sis, but I have a great team, and we all learned from the best—you!"

"The one thing I never would have known to choose would have been this color scheme, Ellie. I love the varying shades of grays and black mixed in with that gentle, *gentle*, muted light blue. It's a perfect blend of softness and strength."

"We kept your white trim so that it wouldn't feel too dark and closed in. It also helped to keep the cost down. We were able to use the desk you already had, and saving money in those areas allowed us to get some of the extra organizers and tools for the craft area. It looked really good already, but now, well, I think it looks *great*!" She looked at Henry. "You haven't said much, Captain Evans. Will this work for you?"

As he opened his mouth to speak, I could see his top lip begin to quiver. He was able to stop the flow of both tears and words by gently pursing his lips together and approvingly nodding his head. He was clearly overwhelmed by the transformation and by all the hard work that had been gifted to us. My dear Henry generously gives time and resources— usually behind the scenes—so being on the receiving end of a makeover of this magnitude left him unable to put his gratitude into words.

We both just stood there. Soaking in the beauty of the room. Soaking in the wonder of the moment.

We posed for pictures and gave many hugs and words of sincere thanks to Molly, Ellie, and the entire crew, stopping first at the window seat that doubled as a daybed with a trundle. Ellie had selected gentle, muted shades of gray and light blue for the bedding, and with the gifted touch of a skilled decorator, she had chosen multiple pillows to surround the sides and back of the daybed. The little nook that had only recently looked so...well, *functional*, now called out to all who passed by to "relax," "read another chapter," and "sit a spell." In fact, Ellie had used my cutting machine to create an adorable gallery of wall art that voiced those very words. She hung the three signs on one of the side walls of the nook and even made them from some of the supplies I already had.

Henry, finally able to speak without fear of all-out crying, said exactly what I was thinking: "I can hardly wait for Kayla and Maggie to get to try this out next week. They may never come downstairs again!"

"I know, right? I designed it, and I confess that I had a hard time not asking to move in here and make this space *my* room!" Many of the crew members, nodding in agreement, joined in on the laughter. "One of the things we wanted to surprise you with was that little mini closet just around the corner from the entry to the bonus room. It's pretty narrow, so it probably won't work for storage, but it *will* give guests a place to hang a few clothes and could maybe hold an upright suitcase or two."

"That was genius, Ellie! Sheer genius!" I'm not sure how many times I said the words *sheer genius* that afternoon, but they certainly applied to Ellie's design throughout the room: the office space, the game table and game storage area, the conversational grouping of the couch, daybed, and overstuffed bean-bag-style chairs, and the craft space.

Ah, that beautiful, well-organized, functional, I-can-hardly-wait-to-use-it craft space!

CHAPTER 45

My mother served an award-winning pot roast for Sunday dinner this week. The smell of the roast, potatoes, and carrots cooking in the Dutch oven greeted us as we walked into my parents' house after church, and the meal itself did not disappoint. Mom cheated this week and bought an apple pie at Hendricksens' Gas and Grocery, but it was as good as homemade! Well, actually it *was* homemade, because Mrs. Hendricksen— another of Dodgeville's amazing cooks— makes them fresh every morning back in the bakery. Mom bought it on Saturday, but because she turned off the oven, dished up the meal, and then put the pie in the oven while we ate, it tasted fresh-out-of-the-oven good!

Oh my heart. That leads me to a rabbit trail, but I simply have to hop on down it, because I know that some of you will be able to relate to it.

When Henry and I were first married, I remembered how good my parents' house smelled when we came home from church on Sundays, and I wanted our house to have that same cozy smell of a home-cooked meal. We were living in a newly constructed house in Connecticut at the time, and we had new appliances installed soon after moving in. I had requested the "Timed Bake" feature, thinking that it would be perfect for timing a pot roast to be done when we got home from church.

Surely some of you have already guessed what happened, because I know that I'm not the only one to have walked in the door, breathed in deeply, smelled absolutely nothing, and then remembered that I hadn't set the timer for the oven!

We ate out that day.

However, in true Bitsy Lee Evans style, the story doesn't stop there! Fast forward to three weeks ago. We invited some friends over for Sunday brunch after the morning service. They were traveling through Dodgeville on their way to Florida and needed to get back on the road as quickly as possible after brunch. Remembering my earlier fiasco with the timed-bake button, I woke up at six o'clock that morning just to set the timer so that that our brunch casserole would be done the minute we walked in the door from church.

Ten minutes before the service, we met our friends on the front steps of Dodgeville Community Church, found our place on the pew behind my parents, exchanged a few howdies, and waited for the service to begin.

We stood for the opening prayer, and it hit me: I had set the timer, but I hadn't put the casserole in the oven! One of these days I'll find the happy medium and get it right!

Oh, and for those of you who are wondering if we ate out that Sunday, I am happy to say that I was able to sneak out before the end of the prayer, head home, put the casserole in, feed Wilbur an extra treat, and make it back to DCC before Pastor Dave stood to speak!

It's definitely one of the benefits of living in a small town!

It's been killing me not to tell you more about the amazing room makeover we got from Ellie and her team at the amazing design firm in Greenville that I've been telling you about.

Wait! Did I tell you that Ellie is Molly's sister? Designer Molly is the one who is doing the phenomenal transformation over at the Sweet Tea and Sunshine Café. The decorator gene clearly plays out strong in their family tree!

So anyhow, I'm going to post a link at the end of this live feed. It will take you directly to Ellie's design page on the firm's website. She posted pictures this morning from our bonus room makeover reveal that took place yesterday afternoon, and y'all are just gonna wish you could fly Ellie to your home state to have her work on your house. She did an *amazing* job and went above and beyond in her attention to detail and in making our bonus room both beautiful and functional. I don't know about you, but when I decorate, I generally end up with one or the other; seldom, both.

We're going to make the signs like the ones you'll see in the daybed nook available on our site soon, so stay tuned! In the meantime, hop on over to Ellie's page and let us know what you think. We love it and highly recommend both Ellie and Molly for any commercial or residential design work you may have.

Today I'm headed to Columbia with my friend Katy to pick hundreds of strawberries for a yummy addition to the Dodgeville Days cuisine! To say that it's getting exciting around town is an understatement!

CHAPTER 46

Henry got in late last night from a quick one-day trip, so he's napping in the other room. Me? Why thank you for asking! I'm whooped! I picked every single strawberry in the state of South Carolina yesterday. Okay, fine. It just felt like it. But...wow! I'm clearly getting old. Bending over and picking berries all day is just not as easy as it used to be. That's why I'm drinking my coffee extra strong this morning. I'm drinking it from my white "Today is going to be 'paw-fect'" mug, aptly chosen for reasons you shall soon see. But first, go grab your coffee or tea, and I'll meet you right back here. Don't worry if it takes a few extra minutes to brew. I'll wait...right here at the end of the old gravel road.

The excitement in Dodgeville right now is literally palpable! Dodgeville Days is this Friday and Saturday, and the people are proving that we really do clean up well around here! Kaleb—the owner and chief barber at Kaleb's Klippers—told me last evening that this is his busiest week of the year, for men and women alike!

We put a lot of heart into Dodgeville Days, and it draws a big crowd from all across the Upstate because of it. In fact, two years ago, we had people from Virginia, North Carolina, Florida, Georgia, and Tennessee who came to town just to attend the festivities—they had no family or friends in town prior to that weekend. I think many of them are planning to return this year.

Since we had to skip last year (2020)— due to something I chose early on not to blog about nor allow to divide my followers—we're all grateful to be back at it, welcoming out-of-towners and letting them know that in Dodgeville, they matter to us.

But in my eagerness to "get the show on the road," I thought this morning about festivals past. The memories are sweet, include many of the same people in each of the same locations year after year, and bring me to tears as I think of some who have passed away since our last one and therefore won't be here as an active part of this year's festivities.

One of my favorite stories from Dodgeville Days is certain to come up in more than one conversation around town this year. It's almost become a festival legend, so I simply have to share it with you today!

By way of reminder—or by way of introduction for those of you just joining our journey down the old gravel road—I was born in Dodgeville. My family moved away when I was ten, but I was born here.

We had a dog—half chihuahua, half Pomeranian—whose name was Chico. (I think because my brother was taking a Spanish class at the time, he chose the name that meant boy*.) Chico was very protective of our family, but he was also extremely sweet. (Let's just say that he let me put bows around his head and dress him in large doll dresses. Poor thing.) He was well trained, well cared for, and well loved.*

The story goes that my mom, Miss Pauline, Grandma Ruth, and a dear woman by the name of Miss Othinel spent three entire days making (and artistically decorating) cookies for the Dodgeville Days Welcome Booth. Trust me, these women could bake with the best of them—even back then!

My parents had recently put an addition on our home, allowing my dad, a pilot, to have some office space where he could study for his various written exams to become licensed on the specific airplanes he flew. He was so proud of that space and probably enjoyed the quiet place to both read and study following his one-day trips to cities across the United States and back.

The addition was just to the left of our entryway, and to separate it from the rest of the house, Mom chose to use an accordion-style door that could be opened easily when they entertained large groups.

Because Dad was traveling the first half of the week of Dodgeville Days that year, his study made the perfect storage area for the nearly one thousand cookies that would make even the fanciest French pastry chef envious. On Friday morning the ladies were to meet at our house to transport the trays of cookies to the booth.

That year, my Uncle Marvin (my dad's brother), timed his visit around Dodgeville Days and stayed in the guest room upstairs. He had driven all night and had arrived just as we were heading out for breakfast with the Dodgeville Days committee—at the Sweet Tea and Sunshine Café.

Mom gave Uncle Marvin the rundown of where his towels and extra toiletries were located. Dad gave him the extra house key. He was going to take a quick shower and join us for a bite of breakfast at Miss P's.

Apparently, sweet, loving, adorable, willing-to-wear-doll-dresses Chico had no idea who Marvin was, stood at the bottom of the stairs, and barked incessantly at the supposed intruder. When it came time for Marvin to leave, Chico wasn't about to let him get near the front door. Though he was small in both stature and ability, Chico's bark was ferociously large. Marvin later confessed that he indeed found himself intimidated by the little guy.

Using his quick, well-trained-lawyer instincts, he reached for the nearest door—the accordion door leading to my father's office—pushed it open, and told the barking guard to "get in there!" He was proud of his speedy problem-solving skills and couldn't wait to share his accomplishments with all of us at breakfast.

*Try as you might, you'll have a hard time picturing the exact amount of speed with which my mother jumped up from the table, grabbed me by one hand, my brother by the other, and hollered back to my father to tell Miss P he would pay her later—she needed him to drive us home...*now!

By the time the untouched-by-canine-tongue cookies were delivered to the booth that morning, the town and most of its guests had heard of the early morning cookie caper at the Halls' house. No, not one covered tray had been bothered. Not one cookie licked, eaten, or otherwise disturbed. It seems that all that barking wore poor Chico out, and he was sleeping soundly, even as Mom threw open the accordion door, screaming for him to, "Stop!"

To this day I remember the puzzled look Chico gave her and the tears of relief that found their way down Mom's cheeks—right before she broke out into the most uncontrollable belly laugh I've heard from her before or since that day.

Uncle Marvin never lived it down. In fact, as my father shared the story at his brother's funeral a few years ago, the memory brought smiles where only tears had been just moments before.

There are no cookies this year, but there will be strawberry pies aplenty! Thank you for laughing with me today as I took this little trip down memory lane...from my desk in the sunroom...at the back of the house...at the end of the old gravel road.

CHAPTER 47

"I don't know *why* he can't get out of bed. I only know that I need you and Henry to help me. I hesitated to call you because I know how busy you are this week with the booth and the café's makeover and all. But I just *can't* get him out of bed on my own. I just don't think it's bad enough that I need to call the medical team over."

"Mom. Slow down. Is he still sitting on the edge of the bed, or did he fall back down into a lying-down position?" Walking as she replied, I put her on speaker so that Henry could hear her as I entered the great room, where he had been taking his morning-after-a-flight nap.

"Is he okay?" Henry whispered with urgency in his voice but gentleness in his volume.

"No. We need to head over right away." My reply was more a shaking of my head, which said more than my words could convey.

"He's on the side of the bed. He's kind of slumped over, like he's passed out, but he's breathing and has a pulse. I checked."

Even after retirement, Mom had kept up with her first aid training. She felt it was important for anyone working at the school to be current on such things, and even though her first aid courses had focused on the basics, the basics were what she needed most in this moment. Actually, her calm response was her greatest asset, but the training ran a close second.

"We're leaving now. Stay on the phone with me. Sing to him, Mom. That worked last time. We'll be there before you know it. But stay on the line in case you need us to do something or to call someone else."

"Okay. But hurry." And with that, she began humming a tune known only to her as she improvised a soothing melody from the resources of her love for my father. Her gentle spirit was even calming *me* over the phone line.

Henry handed me his phone after he buckled his seatbelt. "I already dialed Doc Michaels. Just tell him what's going on."

I muted my phone so that it wouldn't confuse my mom as to who I was speaking to. "Doc, it's Bitsy. It's my dad. I think he's having another one of those episodes. Should we call for the ambulance?"

Though he was relatively young, Dr. Michaels had earned the trust of most of the residents of Dodgeville—the others just hadn't needed his services...yet. He was focused but able to take in the big picture surrounding the illness and the patient.

He was, as Mom had often said, "Big-city trained, but with a small-town heart." These were the times when that shone through.

"I can meet you there. I'm actually only a couple of blocks from their house right now. If you get there first, don't try to stand him up. If anything, help him to lie down flat." And with that, he hung up, grabbed his car keys from the pocket of the jacket he had brought along "just in case it stayed chilly," and headed to Ed and Lori Hall's house, arriving just as we were starting up the porch steps to the front door.

"Perfect timing, Doc." Henry's words held both admiration and gratitude.

I didn't knock. Mom never locked her door, and I was certain that we wouldn't startle her, since she knew we were on the way. Until we knew what was wrong, every second mattered. Additionally, I didn't want her to have to leave Dad unattended.

"Mr. Hall.... Mr. Hall...." When there was no response or even acknowledgement of our presence, Dr. Michaels spoke directly to Henry. "Help me lay him down. I'm going to check his airway after we do that. Let's get him onto his back. Mrs. Hall, will you and Bitsy help lift his legs back onto the bed when we pivot him from the seated position, please?"

Somehow, the four of us worked in unrehearsed but perfect unison, the three of us who were not doctors quickly moving out of the way once our task of assisting was done.

In a relatively short time after Doc Michaels had checked Dad's vital signs and had looked for other indications of the cause for this event, Dad opened his eyes.

"Well, hi, Doc! I didn't hear you come in. Lori," he called out to Mom, "would you get Doc Michaels a cup of your extra-good coffee? He's out awful early this morning."

Dr. Michaels didn't flinch an inch, nor did he take his eyes off of my father. The rest of us, however, exchanged glances and were left speechless by this quick rebound and the easy flow of words that accompanied it.

As quickly as Dad had "frozen," he "unfroze" and seemingly picked up where he had left off. No one really knew what to make of it. It had happened only once before, but this one seemed to have lasted a bit longer than the first. He had been a little harder to "wake" this time too.

Doc summarized it succinctly. "It's a Parkinsonism." The label somehow let us know that this would be our new normal, even though we had come to see that Parkinson's was anything *but* normal. However, it was somehow reassuring to know that, although Parkinson's presents differently in each patient, this wasn't something unknown.

"It's like he's having a type of seizure. But it's reversed from what we normally think: tremors, shaking, biting.... Instead, your dad has almost a 'frozen seizure,' where he is unable to do any of those things, so his body does the opposite and just can't move. For reasons I'm not totally certain of yet, your dad seems to 'unfreeze' if we can help him lie down and get oxygen moving easily through his body. Now, mind you, that's not a medical term by a long shot, but I do think it best describes what's happening."

We were listening. It was just difficult to let it soak in and to know that these would continue—if not even increase in frequency—in the future. Dr. Michaels seemed to sense our need to absorb the realities of this element of the disease, and he continued.

"It may sound contradictory, but don't watch for these 'frozen seizures' or fear their occurrence. However, you should anticipate them. If he doesn't respond right away, call for emergency help. Then call me. Always call the emergency number first, though. Since we don't know yet—and may never know—what triggers these episodes, we can't prevent them at this point. But we can be prepared.

Mrs. Hall, make sure ahead of time that anyone you normally would call knows how to help you. Bitsy and Henry, I heard that your boys are coming to town, so maybe even inform them of how they can help if necessary. Be proactive by keeping a consistent schedule, sticking to your good eating plan, and getting lots of exercise. That exercise is your best friend, Mr. Hall. Keep it up. I'm so impressed when I see you two walking around town, so stick with it!"

"What about the festival? Is that too strenuous, Dr. Michaels?" Mom knew that Dad would insist on being right in the thick of things, serving as the self-appointed greeter to all the visitors to our little town.

"I see no problem in moving forward as planned." He turned his attention to Dad as he completed his answer. "But don't try to set any records for greeting the most people or shaking the most hands, Mr. Hall! It's okay to sit at a table and let the people come to you now and then. With that effervescent smile of yours, they'll never know the difference!"

His gentle hint of humor at the end was the tension breaker that we all needed. It seemed to relax each of us, including Dad.

"Well, Dr. Michaels, I don't know what I'd do without you. 'Thank you' seems trivial. So let me make you a good hot breakfast before you head back over to the office." Mom meant every word of it. For her, gratitude was best expressed with down-home cookin'!

"Thank you, Mrs. Hall, but I've eaten, and I really do need to get a little paperwork done today so that I can enjoy the weekend with all the fine citizens of Dodgeville. Mr. Hall, Captain Henry, Miss Bitsy, I'll see y'all downtown sometime soon. Remember that you can call me anytime—day or night." And with that, he turned and headed to the front door.

As Henry walked Doc Michaels to the door, they spoke in hushed tones. Knowing my Henry, I was sure he was gathering every last drop of help and advice that he could obtain from our one-in-a-million town doctor.

With a plan in place and the appropriate steps to take if this were to happen again (now in writing and placed on the kitchen bulletin board), Henry and I felt comfortable heading home to freshen up before heading over to Miss P's. It was time to switch gears and help Molly with the finishing touches on the décor before the big reveal!

CHAPTER 48

We gave ourselves the morning off today, and after a quick trip to my parents' house to lend a hand with something, we came home and took a gloriously restful one-hour nap. It was just what both Henry and I needed this morning.

But oh. my. heart. The blog post won't go up until tomorrow, but you simply *must* plan a trip to Dodgeville—*soon*! You will not believe the remodel that was just gifted to our little café on the town square. Seriously. It's amazing!

One of Greenville's largest—and best— design firms took on the project, headed by the famous "Decorator Molly," as we all lovingly call her. Her sister Ellie is the one who transformed our previously blah bonus room into our new favorite place in the house.

The café has been in Miss Pauline's care for over forty years. She was an only child, and her parents passed away when she was three, so her grandparents took on the responsibility of raising her. That's a very interesting piece of Dodgeville history that I'll set aside for another day, but to make a long story, well, not as long,

I'll just say that she inherited it from her grandmother when she was twenty-six. She actually started working there after school and on Saturdays when she was in high school. From that time until she became the owner, she always thought it should be called something other than The Dodgeville Diner. The day she took ownership was also the day that it officially became the Sweet Tea and Sunshine Café. The name suits Miss P, the café, and Dodgeville—to a *T*. (See what I did there?)

Why did I tell you that? Oh yes—because we helped Decorator Molly with the finishing touches after our naps this morning, and both Henry and I were blown away! Let's say we did more ooh-ing and ahh-ing than helping!

I'm allowed to give you one teaser, so here it is: sweet tea and sunshine! Seriously, that's your hint! Be sure to catch the blog tomorrow to see how the name of the café plays out in its new décor!

Until then, take a minute to go to our website, *TheOldGravelRoad.com*, and click the link for the Dodgeville Days schedule. We'd love to see you there!

CHAPTER 49

"How's he doing, Mom?"

"Great! When he woke up from his nap, he was determined to ride two more miles on the bike. Allen checks up on your dad's progress every Sunday evening when he and Lydia call. Your dad figures he's logged enough miles on the bike by now to be somewhere in North Carolina. When he finished his ride, he was as fresh as a daisy! Oh— that reminds me: How much do I owe you for our part of the bouquet for the opening this afternoon?"

"I don't have the receipt in front of me, but I'll let you know, and we can settle up after the reception. I asked Miss Janice's daughter—the older one...I can never remember her name...."

"I think that one's Claire, dear."

"No, she's the one who's still in high school. Oh, what is that girl's—Erika. That's her. Erika. She's the one in college. In fact, she's heading out to Arkansas for grad school next year to study horticulture. I guess the nursery business is in her future. Anyhow, I asked Erika to make it as close as possible to the one you ordered for the anniversary party last year. Apparently they keep a record on each customer, and it even includes photos of the arrangements they make for you. She can just pull it up in their online file under your name."

"Ooh, that's good to know. Thanks for taking care of that, dear one."

"No problem. Do you want us to pick you up today?"

"Thank you, but no. We need to grab some groceries and stop by the pharmacy afterward, so we'll just meet you there."

"Okay. I'm glad that Dad's doing well. Now— how are *you* doing? You still have time for a quick nap, you know. I promise I won't tell anyone that you took a midday nap."

Mom would rather be tired than ever confess to needing a nap during the day. I, on the other hand, would rather *take* a nap than have all of my friends wish that I had *taken* a nap! Mom's so sweet though, that no one would know the difference.

"Wouldn't tell you if I *did*!" Her laughter was music to my ears after the morning she had just been through.

"See you there, then. Love you bunches."

"I love you too, dear one. Hugs to Henry."

CHAPTER 50

Today's mug is navy blue, has lettering that pops in a deep shade of true yellow, and says, "For all of our tomorrows...." Henry and I say that to each other often, and he gave me this mug yesterday. I wasn't going to use it—just put it on a shelf for display—but he insisted that I use it, enjoy it, and allow it to remind me of his love. So using it, I am! In a moment, I'll tell you more about the reason behind this sweet gift, but first, go grab your coffee or tea, and I'll meet you right back here. Don't worry if it takes a few extra minutes to brew. I'll wait...right here at the end of the old gravel road.

As I begin today's post, I want to encourage those of you who own or work for big businesses in big cities to respect and honor small businesses in small towns. It not only means the world to the owner; it also speaks highly to those who are watching to see how your company does business.

This past month I have watched as one of the top decorators from one of the top design firms in one of our state's largest cities has embraced the people and businesses of our beloved Dodgeville. She has honored them with her questions, her business, her listening ear, and her time. For this, Decorator Molly, we thank you.

When Henry and I, along with my parents and other invited guests, attended a lovely pre-grand-reopening reception yesterday at the Sweet Tea and Sunshine Café, there were hors d' oeuvres and petit fours artfully and tastefully (no pun intended) presented for the guests to enjoy as they toured the newly remodeled café. These were not purchased from the well-known bakery that makes its home along the main thoroughfare of Greenville's amazing downtown area. No, these were even better than that—they came from the bakery department at Hendricksens' Gas and Grocery, where Mrs. Hendricksen made them from scratch early yesterday morning.

"I don't want to bring the city to Dodgeville," Decorator Molly told me as we stood near the orange-upholstered booths that grace the back left quadrant of the café. "I want to take the values I've seen and the lessons I've learned here back to the city."

And for this, Decorator Molly, we again thank you.

This attitude of openness, humility, and respect was the force behind a café remodel that gave Miss Pauline exactly what she would have asked for—had she known that it was exactly what she had wanted all along.

It's perfect.

Molly's inspiration came from the name of the café itself: Sweet Tea and Sunshine. The orange-tinted sweet tea in Miss Pauline's trademark glass pitchers and the crisp yellow of the lemons and the South Carolina sunshine resulted in a color scheme that most would carry out in a garish or unblended way.

Not Molly and her team.

Where there were once cemented-in walls with only three small windows, closer to the ceiling than to the patrons at the tables under them, there is now a wall of glass. It is perfectly divided into fourths by black metal seams, providing both the support and aesthetic deserved by such a dramatic change.

Actually, let me quickly walk you through the "new and improved" Sweet Tea and Sunshine. Later this weekend, Molly will have pictures of the entire process on her website, so I'll post a link when that's ready. She wants the people of Dodgeville to get to see it first—and that's just another reason we all love her and her team!

Picture a rectangular tissue box, sitting on a table in front of you, with the "long side" facing you. I'm going to use this imaginary box to help you picture the before and after of Miss P's adorable café.

In the "before," with the long side of the box facing you, you would be standing on Main Street. You would see only the outdated siding (running the length of the building), with three, three-feet-long by eighteen-inches-high windows, situated approximately one foot below the partially rusted gutters and perfectly centered within their third of the building.

The entrance was previously on the short side of the tissue box, on the right as you stand looking at it. The door, with "Sweet Tea and Sunshine Café" meticulously stenciled in white on the glass, opened inward from Oak Street and was located at the end that was the farthest from Main Street. It was the only public entrance to Miss P's.

As you entered, the cash register was to the left of the door, meaning that both "comers" and "goers" would vie for a space to either request seating or pay their bills. At times, the line would be outside the door until enough space could clear for the next customer to complete their transaction. Miss P's Dodgeville souvenirs—mugs, aprons, and wall art, among other items crafted by local artisans—were displayed in a crowded but tidy glass case under the cash register. These items were becoming increasingly popular among locals and tourists alike, adding buyers to the already long lines by the door.

For the sake of time, suffice it to say that sweet Miss Pauline was more than ready for some helpful ideas and changes from Decorator Molly and her team.

Actually, let me stop right here and admit that I'm never going to accomplish this in one blog post. There is *too much to tell, and I don't want you to miss a thing! So let me think this through. Hmm....*

I'll post the "after" story this evening as a "Part 2" to this one. By then I should be able to tell you the new town motto that Pastor Dave is going to announce at the opening ceremony tonight.

I'll close Part 1 with Miss P's list of the top ten things she either wanted or needed for her café's makeover:

    1. An additional public entrance/exit
    2. "Gift Shop" area
    3. New booths (bye-bye, duct tape!)
    4. Some "coffee-house-style" seating
    5. A centrally located cash register
    6. Multi-stall bathrooms
    7. A more streamlined kitchen space
    8. A space for pastries and treats
    9. A sweet tea and coffee station
    10. More tables for more customers

Let me add here that Miss P never, and I do mean never, calls people customers. *They are her* guests. *And she treats them accordingly.*

Oh, I nearly forgot to tell you why I chose to drink my coffee this morning from my "For all of our tomorrows" mug.

Yesterday Henry and I celebrated our tenth anniversary, and he chose the colors we used for our wedding as the colors for the mug! I love this man dearly and will continue to love him "for all of our tomorrows." So thank you for being a part of our lives. I personally thank you...from my desk in the sunroom...at the back of the house...at the end of the old gravel road.

CHAPTER 51

"Ben called. They're going to arrive about an hour early!"

"That's probably why Jonathan couldn't get through to you—you were talking to Ben. I was just coming to your office to tell you that Jonathan got an earlier flight. He's arriving *tonight*! He flies into GSP during the opening ceremony, so he went ahead and just rented a car to use while he's here. Oh, Henry, I think I'm going to cry. We're all going to be together—*tonight*!"

"Thank you for lovin' on my boys these past ten years. And an even bigger thank you for loving *me*!" Henry's accompanying hug made his words linger in my mind as I enjoyed yet another of his delightful morning kisses.

"Wait! We don't have time for huggin' and kissin', mister! We've got family coming today, and you need to skedaddle over to Dad's to go fishing."

"And you need to get yourself over to the café. So how many fry pies is Miss P planning to have y'all make this morning?"

"I'm not sure. But I can safely say that Mom, Katy, Miss P, and I will definitely have more fry pies by noon than the number of fish you and Dad will have caught!"

His warm laughter enticed me to offer one more kiss before we headed our separate ways.

"Oh, and there's been a change of plans: I think we'll just have leftovers for lunch. So if you and Dad can meet us back here around noon, we'll plan to eat at 12:15. That will be easier for my parents and for us too."

"We're going to stick pretty close to town. I think your mom and I will both feel better knowing that your dad is near medical care if it's needed." We exchanged a knowing glance. "Yes. I know he's fine, and that it was a rare thing to have that incident yesterday. I also know that it scared the liver out of me to see him like that, and I would just feel better knowing that Doc Michaels is only a short distance away."

"I think that's incredibly wise, my love. I somehow think Mom will like your decision too. Parkinson's is definitely a game changer in the way we do things now."

CHAPTER 52

One question I'm often asked is why my writing doesn't seem to include much "Southern" talk: twang, drawls, extended or added syllables, and such. And honestly, that's a great—and a fair—question!

The answer is simple. In the Upstate, there's *some* Southern twang, *lots* of *y'alls* and *all-y'alls*, and apparently a whole *slew* of people named Honey, Darlin', Sweetie, and Sugar. But the other element present in the Upstate of South Carolina is transplants—as in people who have moved to this region from other areas.

In the Low Country of South Carolina, you'll find more of the "slow Southern drawl" (think Charleston and Beaufort).

Throughout the state—as is true in just about any state—you'll find a mix of accents and a wide range of levels within those accents (minor, thick, slow, fast, and so on).

I personally feel that many Southerners—too many, in my opinion—have *tried* to lose their accent. There has long been a negative stigma attached to the Southern drawl, so in an attempt to avoid appearing ignorant or uneducated, people all across the South have made a concerted effort to "speak more Northern."

However, the unrushed beauty of a Southern gentleman drawing out each syllable to its fullest value and inserting additional syllables so that a simple word may take its rightful place within the conversation is nothing short of exquisite. There is nothing ignorant or uneducated about it.

The hurried, run-on sentences of a Southern mother speaking excitedly to her children or her friend since childhood are similarly beautiful to those of the seersucker-clad gentleman previously described. She is free to fling her syllables about at breakneck speed— not because she doesn't *care* what others think, but because she knows what *she* thinks. And that, my friends, is a wisdom that few of us possess.

So in my writing, as I share stories of my beloved Dodgeville friends and family, I write as *I* speak—which is primarily a scrambled mix of tones from Minnesota,

Virginia, and South Carolina. I wish to do nothing to portray these dear people— *my* people—in a negative light...even if that light is cast by negative assumptions that stem from an uninformed correlation between accents and intelligence.

On that note, just a reminder for *all-y'all* to check back again soon. I'll be posting live from our booth at Dodgeville Days tomorrow with some fun giveaways, and I'll have some video updates that you won't want to miss!

CHAPTER 53

"Katy, I love that idea. How did we not think of this before now?"

"As my Fred would say, 'The timing wasn't right yet.'"

"What are you girls whispering about over there? You're not tryin' to sneak any of those fry pies into your tote bags now, are you?"

Katy and I exchanged glances that made it clear we agreed with one another. It wasn't time to say anything to anyone else yet.

I quickly answered her question: "It's tempting, Miss P. I think this may be the best batch of fry pies we've ever made for 'the Days.' What's different about this dough today? It's so easy to work with."

"My Grandma Ruth always said that the weather made a big difference. 'Make it on a pretty day, and you'll get a pretty pie,' she'd say. She cooked better'n anyone I know, so if she said that's when to do your baking, then that's when I try to do my baking. Then again, you can't just bake on the day you *want* to, or your loved ones would starve!"

We simultaneously began our chorus of giggles—an outward expression of our time-tested camaraderie. Mom, Katy, and Miss P had been making fry pies for Dodgeville Days long before I came back to town, and as I enjoyed the sound of their laughter, I suddenly felt blessed to be included in this gathering of women, influenced by their wisdom, experience, and friendship.

As Katy and I were leaving, each with a bag of fry pies in hand, she said in low tones, "Fred *and Jillian* and I will stop by your booth in the morning!" My knowing smile was her reply.

As mothers are somehow able to do, no matter how old their children are, my mom overheard her comment. Without missing a beat, she took her bag of fry pies with one hand and rested the other on my forearm, while whispering, "I like that idea...a lot. Your dad and I have been thinking that for quite a while now. What took you two so long?"

CHAPTER 54

"Was that a car door?"

"Nope. Still not a car door." Henry was just as eager for the sound to *be* a car door as I was, so he didn't bother to make fun of the question I had already asked three times within that hour!

"I'm so glad Dad caught a couple of fish this morning! That'll give him something to talk about with his buddies downtown tonight. He could hardly wait to tell us when he walked in the door! Well, actually, the first thing he couldn't wait to tell us was that you slid all the way down the large rock on your tookus! He quickly added that you were okay and that, although he was worried about you at first, the look on your face was hilarious!"

"We must have laughed for five minutes straight! I fell. I looked at him. He looked at me. And we both instantly burst out laughing at the expression on the other guy's face! I think because it was so muddy, it broke the sharpness of the fall and helped me to slide instead of hitting with such impact. Surprisingly, I'm not sore at all."

"And for that, I am thankful! Did you get a chance to talk to him about his driving?"

"Yes. He basically admitted that what your mom told you last week is true: his reaction time is slowing down. He opened up, thinking I didn't know about it, and shared that, like your mom said, he is avoiding left turns whenever possible. That, of course, means that instead of going left one block to get downtown, he turns right, then right again, and then right again...followed by one more right turn."

"Seriously? Henry, that's horrible—but at the same time a little funny."

"I agree...on both counts. But it gave me a good opportunity to follow some of the suggestions Dr. Michaels gave me the other day. He recommended that we ask him questions that would make any decisions *his*, not ours."

"Like what?" I interrupted.

"Well, like: What if one of the neighbor kids darted out into the street after a ball? Do you feel like you would be able to react quickly enough?"

"That's a great question. What was his answer?"

"He said that he *hoped* he'd be able to, but he really wasn't certain anymore. So I asked what he would do if Mom Hall had a medical emergency, since turning right to avoid left turns may take longer or may not even be possible."

"And his answer...?"

"He hadn't thought of that. Which is understandable. Your parents are both so positive that they tend to be like most of us and never think that those things will happen to them." Henry walked over to look through the blinds toward the driveway. He shook his head side to side, indicating that Ben's family had not arrived yet. "By the end of our time at the lake, he said, 'Ya know, it may be time for me to stop driving. I'd probably be fine'—I felt like he added that part to convince himself more than to convince me—'but I think I'll talk to Lori about that today. Yep…it's probably time. Henry, I wouldn't wish this Parkinson's on anybody.'"

"Aww, bless his heart. That gets me teary-eyed. That's another major life change for him, but you were so wise to ask the kind of questions that would get him thinking about it on his own. Hey wait, did you hear *that*? I think it really *was* a car door this time!"

Before the last of the remaining three doors had closed on Ben and Izzy's black SUV, both Henry and I were out the door, Wilbur close behind.

"Stop it right now! Who are these grownup girls who rode along with you?"

"Grandma Bitsy, it's me, Kayla!"

"And I'm Maggie! Did you *forget* me?"

"I could *never* forget you—*either* of you!" By this time, all four of them were trying to be the first to give hugs to Henry and me, bumping into each other and side-stepping each other as if we were all part of a poorly choreographed greeting-dance!

"We're gonna be four in Sebtempter!"

"I got some new pink shorts to wear to breakfast tomorrow at Dodgeville!"

"My shorts are blue. That's my favorite color. Did you remember *that*, Grandma Bitsy? And my shirt has a heart on it."

Before I could reply or offer any further comment, the girls were running off to greet Wilbur, whose rapidly wagging tail spoke of his delight at the prospect of having some pint-sized playmates for the next few days.

As Henry helped Ben lift the final two suitcases onto the porch, I slid my arm around Izzy's waist, leaned in close, and whispered, "Do the girls know yet?"

She stepped back with the same speed as the gasp that escaped her lips, giving me a look of bewilderment.

"How on earth did you…?"

"I may never have had children of my own, but I can spot the glow of a pregnant woman's face, even in a crowded room! But don't worry. My lips are sealed. That's *your* news to share!"

"I love that about you, Mama B. In spite of your social media presence, you respect our stories and our privacy."

"*Your* story. *Your* timeline."

"Oh, in the excitement, I didn't answer your question. Yes. The girls know. They don't really grasp all that it means, but they know. They thought the baby would be here the next morning after we told them, so they got tired of waiting! But that's been good, because they haven't really cared about telling anyone. It's like it's no big deal."

"That makes sense."

"They don't know it yet, but we're planning to have them tell the three of you when Jonathan gets here—so act surprised!"

I leaned in one last time as we reached the top step. "How have you been feeling, sweet Izzy?"

"I felt worse with the twins, so that's good. But I'm just now in my third month, so I'll be glad when the second trimester gets underway. I think you were the one who told me about using peppermint oil to help with morning sickness. It didn't work at all with the twins, but it's working like a charm this time! In fact, I've been...."

I quickly asked Henry a question so that Izzy would know not to continue her comment: "Sooo...is everything unloaded?"

"All set!" He held open the screen door for Izzy and me as he spoke. "Izzy, I declare that you get prettier every time I see you. You don't look like a tired mother of twins at all!"

"Hmm...I'll take that as a *huge* compliment, Dad Henry, because most days I feel like a *very* tired mother of twins!"

"Well then, you've come to the right place, because I just happen to know some people who will take good care of lovin' on those little ones for the next few days!"

"Speaking of which.... Grandpa Henry and I have a surprise to show you. We got something new since you were here at Christmas!"

"You're going to love it! Grandpa Henry just showed it to me when we took the suitcases upstairs." Benjamin's attention turned to Izzy next, as everyone else headed for the stairs. "You've *got* to see the bonus room. Even in her most glowing descriptions and perfectly shot photos, Mama B didn't fully convey how amazing the update was to this space!"

As we proceeded up the steps, we could already hear the squeals of joy and the inevitable "claiming" of what seemed to them to be the most exciting element in the room:

"I get to sleep in the trouble bed!"

"No, Maggie, *I* get to sleep in the trouble bed!"

"No you don't. I do." Maggie hurriedly ran to be the first to acknowledge us at the top of the stairs. "Mommy, tell Kayla that I get to sleep in the trouble bed!"

"I think there will be plenty of time for both of you to get a chance to sleep in the *trundle* bed when you visit us." I added what I thought would be the peace-making solution: "Did you know that if you sleep on the daybed part of it on top it's like getting to be the one on the top bunk of a bunk bed?"

"Okay, Maggie, *you* can sleep in the trouble bed." Quick-thinking Kayla jumped at the opportunity to be in the "top bunk!"

"No. *I* want to sleep on the top bed. *You* sleep in the trouble bed!"

Izzy looked over at Henry and shook her head. "Now you can see why I look tired most of the time."

CHAPTER 55

Well, y'all, this is my sixth time to send out a live feed from the opening ceremony at Dodgeville Days. Even though I've been blogging for nine years this month, the first two years we had the blog, I didn't do live feeds, and last year, we didn't get to have Dodgeville days. But here we are—back at it again!

This, my friends, is *my* town. These caring, gentle, hardworking people you see behind me are *my* people. They are the residents of this beloved town that has welcomed all of you with open arms and that welcomes family, friends, and strangers alike to enjoy our annual celebration: Dodgeville Days!

Are any of you here or coming sometime on Friday or Saturday? Let me show you where our booth is for *The Old Gravel Road* so that you have no excuse for not coming by to say howdy! We're counting on it!

The excitement in the air is uplifting, encouraging, and an accurate reflection of the pride Dodgeville's residents take in their town.

Well, that...and the fact that there are no classes for *all* of the Dodgeville schools tomorrow. So of course, the kids are just as eager to celebrate as the adults!

The opening ceremony is about to begin, so I'll keep this short.

Can you see our barber shop, Kaleb's Klippers, behind me? See that open-sided tent in the lot next door to it? That's our booth! And see that cute man standing in the booth? That's my Henry!

Okay, so let's get this show on the road and have a giveaway! If you're here, come put your name in the drawing for the basket at the booth. If you're watching this online, comment with only the word *Dodgeville* in the comments below, and it will enter you into our first drawing—yes, there will be more!—for a basket of Dodgeville apparel: a T-shirt, an apron, and a ball cap! We'll select the winner of this first one by 8:00 tomorrow morning, so enter before midnight tonight, Eastern time! An outside, third-party service will randomly select a winner, and we'll announce it here soon after that!

Oops, Pastor Dave is headed to the center of town to start speaking, so I'd better sign off. See you in the morning—or better yet, I'll see you here at Dodgeville Days!

CHAPTER 56

Miss P and Decorator Molly are literally best friends now. I think they talk on the phone daily, and Molly even taught Miss Pauline how to send text messages! Then one of the servers at the café taught her how to add emojis to the texts, and she's nearly as proud of that as she is of her newly remodeled café!

Even after all these years of blogging, writing a "Part 2" is always tricky for me. I want to go back and add information to Part 1 or insert things I should have told you in the first post. But alas, I'll pick up where I left off in our written tour of the newly remodeled Sweet Tea and Sunshine Café. (And yes, I just used the word alas *in a blog post!)*

Grab your imaginary rectangular tissue box again, because it really does help to picture the new layout of the café. Set it the "long way" in front of you. That is how our Sweet Tea and Sunshine Café looks from Main Street.

Let's enter through the new front doors, now located smack-dab in the center of the long side. In fact, stop and look (through your mind's eye) at the all-

glass front! It's slightly tinted and allows sunshine in without creating "blind spots" for those who are sitting in the café.

Walk into the café with me and look to your right. Can you envision the two rusty-red couches with a three-foot round coffee table between them? You may wait there for your table to be ready, or you may sit there and enjoy a cup of coffee on a chilly morning.

If you simply wanted a to-go pastry or some coffee or sweet tea, you could walk via this "short" center aisle up to the cashier/welcome counter in the center of the café, and then turn right. There, to your right, you'd find the Sweet Tea and Coffee Station directly in front of you. There would be a friendly "barista" to take your beverage order and offer you a free homemade donut hole (or two!) to go with it.

Now walk with me to the end of the aisle, where the counter makes a ninety-degree turn. Take a right, and you'll see the glass counter that houses the artfully presented fresh pastries and homemade pies.

If you decided to stick around instead of taking your order to-go, you could feel free to carry your glass of sweet tea to the counter at the front of that quadrant (between the coffee station and the Main Street window wall). You could choose one of the nine comfortable swivel-top stools that are covered in soft but durable yellow fabric and make yourself comfortable. You could sit and watch the comings and goings on Main Street or talk with friends who stopped by to join you.

But don't get too comfortable. We need to continue our tour. So grab your glass of sweet tea and walk back over toward the Main Street entry. This time, look to your left. Two long rusty-red couches face each other—one with its back to the long center aisle; the other, with its back to the large glass window panels along Main Street. They are complemented by a love seat of the same color centered in the area with its back to the short aisle where you are standing.

Four modern, overstuffed chairs (Miss P called them "mini couches for one...or maybe two skinny folks") are in each of the corners of this quadrant. Two of the three-foot round coffee tables sit in the center and serve two purposes: beauty and functionality.

Let's go outside for a minute. Miss P trusts you, so bring your glass of sweet tea with you. She knows you'll be back!

As you're walking out the door, looking at Main Street, take a left, walk to the corner of Main and Oak, and take a left again. Now, enter the "side" entrance to the café. This used to be the only entrance, and the door was nearer the far end than to Main Street, but now it's centered on the second all-glass wall.

Well, I say it's all glass, but there are black metal supports that give it a feel of both sturdy and modern. Miss P didn't like this part in the artist's rendering of how her café would look. But now she says that it "sharpens things up a bit and makes the glass look clean!"

Enter that door with me. (If you're thinking of the tissue box, this is in the center of the short side, on your right as you're looking at the box.) As you look to your left, you'll notice the Sweet Tea and Coffee Station we already toured. So look to your right this time and see the "table quadrant." This area is designed for—but is not exclusive to—guests ordering breakfast or lunch from the menu. Servers will wait on these tables: a staggered mix of four-foot squares, with seating for four, and four-foot by six-foot rectangles, with seating for six.

These tables may be moved together in any combination to allow for larger groups or gatherings. Since Miss P's is closed in the evenings, the Dodgeville Chamber of Commerce meets at the café on the first Monday evening of every month. It was important to Miss P that they be able to create one large table. Molly giggled as she shared with me what Miss Pauline had told her: "They're often divided enough the way it is...if you know what I mean. I want them to be forced to sit in one large seating area!"

Keep walking down the long aisle, and right in the middle you'll see a semicircular welcome station and cash register area where guests will be greeted, directed to their tables, and pay their bills. Miss P and her host or hostess can see everything from here, which was exactly how she wanted it to be! (If you're thinking of your tissue box, this is located right at the opening where the tissues come out.)

The final quadrant, beyond the welcome station, and to your right, houses six booths, each capable of seating four to six people. Covered in a durable but soft orangey-brown fabric, they are back-to-back: three on one side along the kitchen wall; the other three across the aisle that divides that quadrant. The three that line up along the long center aisle have a thirty-six-inch-high barrier wall that provides a little bit of privacy and "keeps the food clean from passersby" (in Miss P's words).

At the end of the long center aisle is the "Gift Shop" (centered at the end, between the couch and booth quadrants). This is a long glass display case with gorgeous handmade bookshelves behind it (handcrafted for Miss P, at Molly's expense and request, by Denny over at Anderson and Sons), filled with items made by local artisans. Miss Pauline loves her Dodgeville more than anyone I know—and all of us love Dodgeville, so that's saying a lot! She sells Dodgeville-related items and donates the proceeds to help buy equipment or supplies for the three local schools: Clara McBride Elementary, Dodgeville Middle School, and GlenVille High.

Many of you have purchased these items from our website or during your visits to Dodgeville, and we are more than grateful for your support of our little town.

Before I close, I'll have to share that I read this description to Miss Pauline to get her approval before I posted it. She asked me to be sure to tell you that she now has multi-stall bathrooms just down from the Gift Shop area. "That's important, since that's one of the things the locals asked for. I guess they didn't like having to wait in the hallway, so I asked Molly if we could spring for a couple of extra stalls! If that's a little thing I can do to make the Sweet Tea and Sunshine Café a haven for people to come to, then extra stalls it is!"

Which is precisely why Pastor Dave's announcement as emcee of tonight's opening ceremony for Dodgeville Days made sense to all of us and received a four-minute ovation. Via a unanimous vote of the City Council, the Chamber of Commerce, and the Board of Citizens, the new town motto for our beloved Dodgeville is: "Dodgeville, SC—where you come first!"

And that, my friends, is a wonderful description of a town that you should come check out for yourself. Its truth makes my heart smile...from my desk in the sunroom...at the back of the house...at the end of the old gravel road.

CHAPTER 57

"Where *is* that boy? I thought he texted you that he had landed right as Pastor Dave started to talk."

"It does take a *little* time to drive here from the airport. And he mentioned something about running 'a quick errand' before he got here, so I'm sure he'll arrive soon. Ben, have you heard anything more from your brother?" Henry knew that if there were any more information to be had, Ben would have it.

"Actually, I let him know at the end of the ceremony that Izzy was taking the girls home to get them to bed, so he'd have to see them in the morning. But I did get a text a few minutes ago that he was on his way. I think that gives us time to get home, and I can let him know that we'll just meet him there."

"Perfect. Henry, will you help me load this empty bin into the back of the car? Then, well, I think that's the last box, so we're good to go for tomorrow!"

CHAPTER 58

"Mama B, why are you crying?"

"Jonathan, have you never met her? She cries at deodorant commercials!" Ben knew I couldn't and wouldn't get upset at his comment, since I often said that very thing about myself!

Izzy teasingly jabbed her elbow into his side. "Oh, come on now, Benjamin, give her a break. That was pretty exciting news Jonathan just shared."

Henry gave Jonathan a thumbs-up, accompanied by a slow-motion nod of approval, and I headed across the room and gave him a wraparound hug.

"Tell us more," Izzy begged.

"No, tell us *everything*!" I added.

CHAPTER 59

Already this morning we met Debbie from New Jersey, Carla from Michigan, Hannah from Tennessee, Janene from Indiana, and...oh, I knew I shouldn't have started this. I'm certain to leave someone out, and your visits to Dodgeville mean so much to us.

To each of you—welcome!

We got to the booth early this morning, and soon we're heading over to Miss P's for a late breakfast. I heard that the lines were pretty long, but we promised our grandgirls some of Miss P's fabulous waffles with strawberries and whipped cream on top. That's their favorite breakfast treat! I'll drop some pictures of it later today.

But be warned: you're going to want to jump in your car and drive to Dodgeville—just for the waffles and strawberries. Or if you're extra hungry, order The Mayor Thompson Platter.

Our former mayor loves Miss P's chicken and waffles, and he always orders a side of fried potatoes, a slice of thick-slab bacon, a sliced tomato, and a dish of strawberries, peaches, or apples (depending on the season) to put on top of his waffle or to eat plain. He told so many of his friends about it that Miss P made it a regular menu option. Just remember that it doesn't come with syrup, so you'll have to request that!

You see, Miss Pauline's Grandma Ruth apparently made the best maple syrup—from scratch. When Mayor Bob was growing up, he and his dad would have breakfast every Saturday at what was then called The Dodgeville Diner. He used to slather his waffles in Grandma Ruth's syrup. I've heard that he even was known to ask for a small empty bowl when he placed his order. He would finish his large waffle—or two, if his dad was feeling generous—pour the remaining syrup from his plate into the empty bowl, and then drink the syrup straight from the bowl.

When Miss P took over the café, she never seemed to be able to master the technique of making the syrup, so she switched to the "store-bought" kind. Mayor Bob, a young adult by that time, vowed not to eat "that syrup with a picture on it" (or any other syrup *not* made by Grandma Ruth), and he's kept his word. Now he'll only eat fruit on his waffles, and he and Miss P continue to have an ongoing, lighthearted "battle of the waffle toppings."

So that's why The Mayor Thompson Platter *doesn't* come with syrup. The menu even has a note that syrup is not included but may be requested, at no extra charge.

The weather is amazing for our first full day of Dodgeville Days! There's an ever-so-slight chance of rain late this afternoon, but it won't affect the fried chicken dinner over in the gymnasium at the Dodgeville Middle School. That dinner is one of the top must-do events during Dodgeville Days every year. I'll tell you all about it in this afternoon's blog post!

Okay, well, there's a crowd gathering here at the booth to watch me do this live feed, so I'm going to flip the camera around and let y'all say howdy to one another! Here goes…!

CHAPTER 60

"Jillian, we're so glad you're joining us for breakfast this morning!"

"Are you Uncle Jonathan's girlfriend?" Kayla and Maggie nearly spoke in unison as they eagerly asked their question, one to Jonathan, the other to Jillian.

"We're working on that," was Jonathan's quick and wise reply. "Now, who wants to get in line for some waffles?"

As soon as she saw me, Katy released her hand from Fred's and made her way over to my spot in line. We asked each other, "Did you know about this when we talked yesterday?"

Our reply mirrored its question's simultaneous response: "I didn't have a clue!"

Mom, standing next to me in line, chimed in, "I guess the secret's out. Now I can *finally* talk about it with someone other than your father."

"Wait! You knew? You knew that Jonathan and Jillian and have been talking?"

"Talking, dating, writing, corresponding, texting—whatever it is they're calling it these days. Yes, I knew. Jonathan made me promise not to tell either of you ladies—or your husbands—and I figured that if I wanted to maintain my top-secret-clearance status, I'd better keep my word!"

"But how…? When did he tell you about this?"

"It was when he was home for Christmas. Do you remember when that large group of old high school friends went out for pizza over in Glenbrook?" Both Katy and I nodded. "It was that night. Jonathan dropped something off at the house afterward—I can't even remember what it was now—and he had that far-away look in his eye that Allen had when he came home and told me about Lydia. I don't know what it is. It's just a look that a young man gets when he's been bitten by the love bug."

Even though Mom was standing right there beside us, Katy looked at me and said, "Your mom is adorable."

"She's also sneaky!" I turned my attention back to Mom. "Secrets have always been your thing, so that doesn't surprise me nearly as much as Jonathan's announcement that he had stopped by to see Jillian on his way home from the airport last night." Turning my eyes back to Katy, I quickly added, "And we were tickled pink, by the way!"

"Imagine *my* surprise when Jillian stayed all dolled up after we got home from the opening ceremony and told us that Jonathan Evans would be stopping by for a few minutes. Fred literally walked over and high-fived her!"

"Now you girls are going to have to contain your excitement and let things happen as they will. Don't put any added pressure on these two kids. They need time, love, and support, and I know that's what you'll give them."

"How did you get so smart, Mom?" I topped off my rhetorical question with a kiss on her forehead before reaching over and squeezing Katy's hand in an understood gesture of my excitement for—and approval of—Dodgeville's newest "couple."

CHAPTER 61

This afternoon as I write, I'm drinking sweet tea rather than coffee. It seemed like the right thing to do, and I'll explain why in a minute. But first, go grab your coffee or tea, and I'll meet you right back here. Don't worry if it takes a few extra minutes to brew. I'll wait...right here at the end of the old gravel road.

Please don't grow weary of my telling you all about Dodgeville Days! It's the biggest event in our little town every year, and it just fills me up for the year ahead. It also reminds me why I love to share our stories with you. I figure that if you can't be here for "the Days," then reading about them is the next best thing!

Family. *That's one of the top four things I love about this weekend. If at all possible, our entire family gathers in Dodgeville on this weekend each year, celebrating birthdays, anniversaries, and memories of treasured moments from the past year. My brother and his wife were unable to make it this year, and we know they would love to be here. However, they also know that we're grownups now, so that means having to do the grownup things: like work and schedule vacation time when its available, not always when we want it to be. Somehow, I think the fact that both Allen and Lydia are in the medical field only makes the scheduling aspect a little trickier than it is for the rest of us.*

We laugh, cry, reminisce, look ahead, eat too much, walk a lot, take naps, stay up late, buy memorabilia, and go to church. We do it together, and that's the part we look forward to and that we remember for years to come.

Friends. *We don't really have class reunions in Dodgeville. We have Dodgeville Days. Perhaps because Dodgeville High School and Glenbrook High School consolidated a few years back, the numbers at the official reunions were decreasing each year. Now most of the graduating classes gather in predetermined areas of the middle school gym for the fried chicken dinner. This became such a popular method for classmates to renew old friendships that a few years ago, the Dodgeville Days planning committee asked the reunion committees to reserve time slots for their dinners. The scheduled gatherings run like clockwork now, helping to overshadow the awkward memories of seven years ago when they ran out of fried chicken!*

The multigenerational and multiethnic gatherings around town include all of us—even those who didn't graduate from a Dodgeville school. If you didn't know anyone here before you came, you're certain to leave Dodgeville Days with the information of new friends in your phone's contact list. As you stay in touch throughout the year, you'll likely plan when and where you're going to meet up when Dodgeville Days rolls around again.

Does it sound too idyllic? Too much like a television sitcom with only nice people and sunny days? That's one of the things we quickly came to love about Dodgeville. It's not perfect. The people aren't perfect. What makes Dodgeville a haven for residents and visitors alike is well summarized in our new town motto (that I told you about briefly in my last post): Dodgeville, SC — Where you come first!

There has long been a mentality of caring about your neighbor, helping someone in need, and giving back to the community that gives so freely of its time, energy, and love to you. This can't be faked. It cannot merely be idealized through the written word. It's real. It's learned. Then it's taught—by example. And then it becomes a lifestyle.

Thinking of others is taught in the schools. In the churches. In the community. But mostly, it's taught in the homes around Dodgeville.

My dad has a saying that fits here: "Be the same person on both sides of the door." In other words, be in front of your children who you are in front of your neighbors, your colleagues, and the person sitting next to you at church. When you remember that you're not perfect, it's hard to expect others to be perfect.

And that's where friendships blossom—at the point of acceptance, understanding, and caring that says, "Yes, I matter, but so do you, so let's learn from each other." And one of the points where friendships flourish best is during Dodgeville Days each year.

Food. *I need to head out to the fried*

chicken dinner soon, so I had better reel in my rabbit trails a bit. Suffice it to say that our little town is blessed with some mighty fine cooks. They would be the first to tell you that if you're looking for a chef, head to Greenville, Columbia, Charlotte, or Atlanta. But if you're looking for a good cook, look in the homes and restaurants of Dodgeville!

I've told you about Miss P's incomparable macaroni and cheese, peach cobbler, and waffles, but I simply must take a moment to tell you about Pop O'Neal's fried chicken.

Several years ago, during Dodgeville Days, then basketball coach Gary O'Neal invited the team to his house for dinner since everyone had the day off from school. His wife made potato salad, bought some pretzels, and picked enough strawberries to feed all the teams in the county. She served the berries on homemade shortcake. Coach was in charge of the fried chicken.

Unbeknownst to anyone in Dodgeville—including Coach's wife, Jenny—Coach O'Neal was very skilled in the culinary arts. His mom had figured that "with his single-minded focus and perfectionist tendencies," he'd never marry, so she taught him the finer elements of cooking, particularly in the area of using spices.

Well, when Coach whipped up his fried chicken for the team, word quickly spread that the team had loved it—even the picky eaters. Their mothers were calling for the recipe; the school's cook even asked for it. But the coach didn't give it out. He said he hadn't quite perfected it and wanted it to be perfect before he shared it.

Fast forward three years after that, and Coach O'Neal—at this point in his final year of teaching and coaching—wanted to leave new uniforms for the next coach to present his team the following year. Coach and Jenny talked about it and decided to put on "a little fundraising dinner" during Dodgeville Days to earn money for the uniforms.

Well, they knew they couldn't do it on their own, so Jenny approached her mom, Fern, to see if some of the ladies from the LMF (Ladies' Missionary Fellowship) down at Dodgeville Community Church would be willing to lend a hand. Fern came back a few days later with a proposal: the ladies would *help if half of the funds raised would be sent to the children's home in Kenya to buy new sports equipment there.*

They struck a deal, and the rest is history. It's as simple as that.

Well, kind of.

The SAA (Student Athletic Association) and the LMF continue to work side by side, evenly dividing the profits between the athletic departments in the Dodgeville schools and the children's home in Kenya. Watching the athletes work so willingly with their "adopted grandmas" from the Ladies Missionary Fellowship is nothing short of inspirational. However, preparing a dinner of this magnitude has become a monumental task. In fact, two years ago, Pop O'Neal (the team changed his title to "Pop" after his retirement), his crew of volunteers from the SAA, and the ladies from the LMF hand dipped, coated, and fried fifteen thousand *pieces of chicken!*

They plan to "fry up" a little over eighteen thousand *this year!*

I wouldn't dare leave this section on food

without a proper shout out to the sweet tea. It flows plentifully during Dodgeville Days and is free at little "Sweet Tea Stations" all around town. (Hence, the sweet tea in my glass as I write. Coffee just didn't feel right today.) Each station sports disposable glasses (or you can bring your own glass canning jar from home), ice, sweet tea, and a host or hostess to both greet and pour.

Fun. *It's not the least element; I'm simply listing it last, because you absolutely* must *come experience it for yourself! There are activities for all ages and rocking chairs all over the place. The townspeople bring theirs from off their porches as a gesture of kindness to visitors, and the committee chairperson always reminds people: "Be sure your address is on the bottom of the chair and be sure to come pick them up on Saturday night after 8:00!"*

So come join us, won't you? I'm headed back downtown, so for now I'll say goodbye...from my desk in the sunroom...at the back of the house...at the end of the old gravel road.

CHAPTER 62

"We get to eat supper with Captain Grandpa and Captain Grandma today!" Maggie loved my parents and thought it was pretty special that she and her twin sister were now old enough to go eat with their great-grandparents all by themselves.

"And *then* do we get to tell our secret, Mommy?"

"Yes, Kayla. When Daddy and I take you over to their house, we can tell them our secret."

"No. *We* don't tell them," she replied, gesturing back and forth between herself and Izzy. "*I* tell them. And Maggie does too. But not you and Daddy. It's *our* secret. Remember, Mommy?"

Izzy looked at Ben with a plea for help. She was plum tuckered out from walking so much yesterday and just didn't have it in her to reason with a nearly four-year-old child this afternoon.

"I've got ya covered." He winked at his tired but radiant wife before heading over to where Kayla and Maggie were sitting on the daybed. There he reminded them that Uncle Jonathan, Grandpa Henry, and Grandma Bitsy would be there too.

With great excitement in his voice, as though coming up with the most wonderful plan in the history of ever, Ben had the girls rehearse the cue for when they would say together, "We're gonna be big sisters!"

CHAPTER 63

"It's been so nice to have you home this week, Henry. A girl could get spoiled having such a handsome fella around all the time."

"I wouldn't have missed a minute of it! And you know I love every minute spent with you."

"Weren't the twins adorable tonight when we dropped them off at Mom and Dad's? They made their little announcement as if they had practiced it for hours."

"I think they had. Ben said it was his way of giving Izzy time to take a nap this afternoon!"

"Mom and Dad loved having the girls all to themselves for a bit tonight. Since Jonathan and Ben were grown by the time my parents added any 'grandchildren' into the family, I think they kind of like having the young ones around."

A few minutes of silent reflection and gratitude filled the room—and our hearts—before Henry spoke again: "Do you ever regret that—not having children of your own?"

"You know that I always wanted children—lots of them! But in some ways, I had that when I taught for a few years. I felt like I got to make an impact on young lives. But no, it wasn't the same. When I started writing for the paper and then got my own column, I felt that as the years went by, my chances for having children of my own were growing smaller with each birthday. Then when the doctor found what he thought was cancer and I had surgery, it settled the answer to the possibility of someday giving birth to children of my own."

"You've been an incredible mom to Jonathan and Ben."

"I can honestly say that I'm grateful they were old enough to have had some sweet memories with Liz before she passed away. And I'm glad for the years you had with them on your own. Your bond is strong, and though I probably won't say it right, your having that relationship with them makes me feel as if they truly *are* my boys—they're just a natural part of who *we* are. I told you that wouldn't come out right."

"I think it came out just fine. I know exactly what you mean, and I'm so grateful that they have you, that I have you, and that we all have each other."

"Why Henry Evans, that was beautiful. Maybe *you* should have been the writer."

"No thanks. I'll stick to airplanes...and you!"

CHAPTER 64

Henry's feeling extra generous this morning, so we're giving away *two* baskets of Dodgeville souvenirs at the booth today. Be sure to stop by and enter the drawing. Henry and I will be here until eleven o'clock this morning, and we'd love to meet you in person.

Have you been over to Miss P's yet? Remember that she's got different hours than some of you have in the city. She's open Monday through Saturday from six in the morning until two thirty in the afternoon.

Miss P had the work-life balance aspect integrated into her café long before it became a "thing." She likes her employees to have time with their families or their friends in the evenings, and always says, "They need to go to church on Sundays—and so do I. I'd be a mess all through the week if I didn't have my church time on Sundays."

Y'all keep asking me for her mac and cheese recipe, and I promise you this: I've tried! Oh how I've tried to get that recipe. But it's a no-go. "I love you like my own, little Bitsy," she'll say all syrupy-sweet-like. But the syrup turns to vinegar when she ends with, "but I'm *not* givin' you my recipe! You'll get it when I'm gone."

The only thing she'll say about it for now is this: "The key's in the buttermilk."

Her employees don't even know the recipe. She makes it herself at four thirty every morning. Then she covers the pans, puts them in the cooler, and brings them out at 10:00 to "let them acclimate to room temperature" before staggering their baking times for the lunch rush.

I confess that I've been known to go in and order two side dishes of mac and cheese and eat just that for my lunch. It's seriously that good.

Be sure to tell her that you heard about her through *The Old Gravel Road*. She often makes it a point to say, "One of *your people* came into my café yesterday."

There are vendor booths all over Dodgeville right now. If you like truly unique handmade items, then you need to get here soon. There are homemade candles (the fragrances are very fresh, and the wax is apparently safe to burn).

There are quality and affordable antiques in the booth next to ours. There's a lady here who will hand-letter signs or note cards for you. There's local honey, loose-leaf tea, gourmet coffee, and baked goods aplenty.

Y'all come! And hurry up about it!

CHAPTER 65

Drinking sweet tea from a glass canning jar just makes it taste better for some reason. So as I write this today, I'm once again enjoying sweet tea, and this time it's in my newest jar, which sports a little handle and even came with a reusable yellow-and-white-striped straw. In a little bit, I'll tell you where I got it, but first, go grab your coffee or tea, and I'll meet you right back here. Don't worry if it takes a few extra minutes to brew. I'll wait...right here at the end of the old gravel road.

First, let me answer a question that was asked several times yesterday: "Why are you taking time to write a blog post when you should be over enjoying Dodgeville Days?" The answer is simple.

I'm a blogger, yes. But I'm also "Mama B" to our boys and "Grandma Bitsy" to our grandgirls. So when the girls needed to take their afternoon nap yesterday, I wanted the rest of the family to be able to participate in the cornhole tournament downtown, so I volunteered to come home with the girls, get a blog post update written, and even sneak in a short nap myself.

Our boys made it to the quarterfinals in the cornhole tournament, so the girls and I will repeat yesterday afternoon's nap schedule and head over in time to see them in the semifinals—if they make it.

Let me answer what I foresee as being today's number one question: Why didn't I participate in the cornhole tournament? If you saw me toss a bean bag, you'd understand. End of story!

Henry and my dad entered too, but they didn't make it into the quarterfinals. They had fun, and that was the goal for this year.

Anderson and Sons Hardware sponsors the cornhole tournament each year. They have cornhole kits made up to sell at Dodgeville Days, and they typically sell out. Denny told me a few weeks ago that he and his son and grandson had handcrafted nearly forty kits this year. They start making them right after Christmas. Denny's wife, Carol, makes the bean bags with her daughter-in-law's help.

I can't remember if I've ever told you this, but their daughter-in-law is

Stephanie, Dr. Michaels's assistant. She is seriously one of the most organized women I know! I even had her come help me organize my kitchen a few years back. "Functionality is the key," she taught me. "It's all about functionality."

Denny's grandson is Kaleb, who owns Kaleb's Klippers. He was pretty busy at the barber shop and didn't think he'd be able to learn to help make the kits. However, his grandpa said, "Kaleb, if you can cut hair, you can cut this wood, so pick up that board and give us a hand over here." The rest is history. Denny and his son Jay get requests for the kits all year long over at the hardware store, but they only make them available during Dodgeville Days.

"We owe that wisdom to Katy," Denny added. "She helped us see that if we 'overmake' them, we'll undersell them. Only making them available during Dodgeville Days makes them, as she says, 'a hot-ticket item.'"

Sweet, sweet Katy. I seriously believe that Dodgeville would be lost without her help, and we're all quick to admit that.

Even though her training in marketing was cut short following the sudden death of her in-laws, Katy has continued to learn the latest and most innovative marketing techniques and utilizes her skills to help the shop owners around Dodgeville.

Mayor Phillips, who was elected after Mayor Bob retired, says, "Katy Liddle can't see into the future, but she sure can tell us how to get there." She's played a vital role in the planning and implementation of Dodgeville Days since she and Junior first moved back here. She set up the website for Dodgeville Days, and she has been a huge help to Henry and me with The Old Gravel Road *site.*

Two years ago, the town honored her at Dodgeville Days by proclaiming July 1, 2019, as Katy Liddle Day and by naming her to be the grand marshal for the July Fourth parade that year. It was such a fitting way for the town to honor this dear woman who has given her skills, talents, and abilities so freely to the community. I doubt I'll ever forget Fred driving her down Main Street in that brand-new bright-red convertible as she simultaneously blushed and beamed while waving at the onlookers. We definitely love sweet Katy around here.

There's still time to join us this afternoon for playing games, shopping at the vendors' booths, enjoying yummy treats from the food trucks, and drinking sweet tea. Be sure to stick around for the closing ceremony. Pastor Dave gives away the prizes people have been signing up to win all weekend, so it's a fun evening that ends the festival on a sweet note.

Oh, speaking of sweet, I said I'd tell you about my new glass canning jar with the handle and the yellow-and-white-striped reusable straw. Decorator Molly and her crew came over for Dodgeville Days yesterday, and she brought one for me and one for Henry. Isn't she the sweetest?

If I sign off now, I'll have time for a quick nap before I run the grandgirls back over for another try (or seven!) at the ring toss. They are determined to win a forty-nine-cent key chain at a dollar a try! So I'll say, "See you later," from my desk in the sunroom...at the back of the house...at the end of the old gravel road.

CHAPTER 66

I've watched Bitsy do this enough times that I think I know how to do it by now, so here goes nothin'!

I literally just stole Bitsy's phone right out of the booth. I told her that maybe we should both put our phones aside and "be present" for the remainder of Dodgeville Days, so I know she won't be looking for it until after the closing ceremony.

Hey, I said I wouldn't use *my* phone. I didn't say I wouldn't use *hers*!

Besides, I had to let you all in on a secret. All I can say for now is that I'll be back online, live, at six thirty Eastern time tonight. Bitsy thinks she's helping Pastor Dave emcee the closing ceremony, but, well...just be here to watch!

Okay, that's all I can say. Oh, other than the fact that I should tell you that I'm Henry, Bitsy's husband! I guess you may want to know that part since I confessed to stealing her phone and all!

See you later—our boys made it into the semifinals for the cornhole tournament, so I think I can keep her occupied over there. In other words, she won't be answering any of your messages until later. I'll be back at six thirty!

CHAPTER 67

"Daddy, since Maggie and I won at the ring toss and you and Uncle Jonathan didn't win the cornhole game, we decided that we want you to have our key chains." Kayla spoke compassionately as she handed him her good-as-gold trinket, while Maggie handed hers to her uncle.

The proud uncle hugged both of the twins as he accepted their generous tokens of kindness. "You girls are the best!"

"We're sorry you're not the best." Maggie wasn't quite certain why her sincere reply evoked laughter from the adults at the table.

"Well I, for one, am just tickled pink that all of us are here together to enjoy these ribs from Smokey's BBQ Truck. Having you all here has meant the world to us." My gratitude was about to spill out my tear ducts, so I was grateful when Dad chimed in.

"I missed having Allen and Lydia here this year, but hopefully we'll all be together this Christmas. And who knows," he spoke with a glance toward Jonathan, "maybe we'll have added more than just a new baby to the family by next year at this time!"

"Grandpa Ed!" Jonathan chided; Jillian blushed.

Henry jumped in to ask if anyone had left room for ice cream, using his question to put a halt to what could only get more awkward this early in Jonathan and Jillian's relationship.

"Sure!" Jonathan quickly replied.

"Absolutely!" Ben's answer was as enthusiastic as his brother's had been only seconds before.

"Like father, like sons. But I'm afraid I'm going to have to pass. I'm stuffed!" Jillian's reply set off a chain of "Me too," from the rest of us—all the way from the oldest down to the two youngest.

"Captain Grandma, can we go look at the petting zoo one more time? I love the baby cows. They're sooo cute."

"They're called *cats*, Kayla. *Cats*."

"No, honey, they're called *calves*. One is a *calf*." Mom, the quintessential librarian and teacher, emphasized the final sound of the *f* as she spoke. "But if there is more than one, then they are called *calves*," with her emphasis on the *v* this time.

"Calves?"

"Yes, Kayla, *calves*. And yes, Maggie, we can go see the calves. That won't take us very long, and I'll bet Captain Grandpa would even be able to walk over there with us." She looked to Dad for his reply.

"I think this old guy can handle that. And with such pretty ladies by my side, I may even be able to talk one or two of them into holding my hands to keep me steady on my feet."

"I'll hold your hand, Captain Grandpa!"

"Me too! I'll hold this one." Kayla grabbed Dad's free hand in hers, and off they went toward the petting zoo area near the gazebo at Dodgeville Community Church.

"Well, ladies, I'll let you two enjoy the quiet for a bit. I guess I'm supposed to help Pastor Dave with a few of the logistics for the closing ceremony, so I'd better head over there. I need to swing by the art fair at the elementary school first, since I promised a few of my grade-oners that I'd go look at their paintings, and they *will* ask me next week if I saw them. Would you girls just see to it that everyone gets over to the ceremony on time?"

Jillian and Izzy were content to sit at the table and enjoy a final glass of sweet tea. "No problem. Do you want us to save you a seat?"

"That would be great." Somewhere over on the left, if possible. Dad hears better out of his right ear."

CHAPTER 68

This time I'll start with an introduction. I'm Henry Evans, Bitsy's husband, and she has no idea that I'm streaming this. But I'm so ridiculously proud of her in this moment, and I know you all played a big role in what's about to happen.

Actually, I'm *always* proud of my dear wife. She used to tell the boys, "I'm always proud of you. I just like it best when other people get to see why." That's sort of how I feel tonight!

Here...I'll flip the camera to record in the direction of the stage. As you can see, we're right in the center of the town square. The stage is encircled by folding chairs, two sets of bleachers brought over from the middle school, and folding lawn chairs in an array of beachy, striped, solid, and tie-dyed patterns of every shade and hue.

Oh...here comes Pastor Dave up to the platform right now!

"Good evening, Dodgeville and friends!"

"Good evening, Pastor Dave!"

"I often end the closing ceremony with a list of those who have worked hard to make this weekend possible. And I plan to do the same tonight. But I'm going to start with a thank you that has been several years in the making. In fact, it's been nearly *nine* years in the making.

"You see, it was nine years ago that Dodgeville's own Bitsy Evans returned to her hometown after having moved away when she was ten. By this time, she was married, an established and well-published writer, and a step-mom to Henry's two grown sons.

"The Evanses bought the house that had been bequeathed to Miss Pauline by her Grandma Ruth, who had it built a few years before then on a piece of land at the end of the old gravel road that got overlooked by the pavers back when the town roads went from gravel to pavement. The house was much larger than Grandma Ruth ever intended it to be and was therefore much larger than Miss Pauline needed. Besides, Miss P wanted to stay in town, closer to the café her grandmother had also left her.

"The house sat empty for all those years, and when Bitsy and Henry came to town to look for a place to call home, Miss Pauline made them an offer they couldn't refuse. And no, none of us know exactly what that deal was!

"As Henry Evans was talking to Jay Anderson on the phone one evening, he gave him the easiest directions to their new home that he could think of: 'We're the house at the end of the old gravel road.' It stuck.

"It was at that time that Mrs. Evans started her blog, *The Old Gravel Road,* which is not only read by thousands but is loved by them as well.

"Mrs. Evans has honored our heritage, our town, our townspeople, and our values by sharing our stories with the world. She has never written a word to belittle us or to make people look bad. She has kept our secrets secret, and she has asked the world to rejoice with us over our smallest accomplishments."

"True to who she is, Mrs. Evans thought she was up here tonight to help me hand out prizes to the winners of our drawings —which I will still need you to do, Bitsy! But we want first to honor and thank her for her gracious promotion of our town.

"Before I continue, let me just stop and ask how many of you are here tonight because you learned about Dodgeville by reading or following *The Old Gravel Road*. Will you just raise your hand up high so that we can see it?

"I'd say that's about a third of you. This visual display makes it clear to all why this year's Dodgeville Citizen of the Year is Mrs. Bitsy Evans. Mayor Phillips, will you please join me on the stage as we congratulate Mrs. Evans?"

"As your elected mayor of Dodgeville, South Carolina, I hereby proclaim Thursday, July 1, 2021, as Beulah Lee Hall Evans Day. (And yes, folks, that's really her official name!) Additionally, I request that Mrs. Evans and her husband, Henry, serve as the grand marshals for the Fourth of July Parade, which will actually be held on Saturday, July third, this year."

Do you hear that applause? That's all for my girl! And I know that Bitsy would want me to thank each of you for your support, encouragement, and loyalty to *The Old Gravel Road* and its various social media platforms.

We are here because of you, with you, and for you. So goodnight, from Dodgeville, SC—where you come first!

CHAPTER 69

Dear, dear...readers? No. Followers? No. Friends. Yes, that's it. Friends.

Dear friends. That's who you are to me. It would feel wrong for me to pillow my head tonight without telling you how grateful I am for you. In fact, I am foregoing my standard opening so that we may simply have a heart-to-heart for a moment or two.

The house is quiet at this hour after a few busy days celebrating the town of Dodgeville. Henry was able to be home all week. The boys were here. Our daughter-in-law was here. Our grandgirls were here. My parents were very much a part of the festivities, and we were able to enjoy extra time with them as well.

While I say that we celebrated the town of Dodgeville, it actually went deeper than that. Dodgeville is home. The people of Dodgeville make it so. Their laughter, care, compassion, helpfulness, can-do spirit, grit, and grace inspire me to share their stories with the world— with you.

I am grateful that they allow me to. I am equally grateful that you want *me to.*

After all, their stories are not unlike your own. They work hard, do hard things, face hardships. They cry, laugh, worry about their children, feel lonely, and mourn the loss of loved ones.

Yet with the same determination you find deep within you in those times, they keep moving forward. They laugh, form friendships, and love from the very depths of their souls. They start over or simply pick up where they left off. They never give up.

They walk beside you so that with ease they can take your hand, lift you up, or have your back within an instant of when the need arises.

Tonight, they welcomed me home. Oh yes, they officially did that when Henry and I moved here nine years ago. But tonight was different.

Tonight, through a sweet honor bestowed upon me, they welcomed not only me, but all of you. In accepting my desire to inspire you with the everyday joys and obstacles of all that is

Dodgeville, they accepted you tonight as well. They let you know that you are welcome here—whether through a physical visit, a live feed from the town square, or a blog post written from within the walls of my sunroom.

Not only have you been invited. You have been welcomed.

For this I am grateful—not just for my townspeople's gracious acceptance of you, but for your acceptance of the people of Dodgeville. You are indeed my friends, and you are loved, and this thought creates within me an overwhelming sense of gratitude tonight as I sit at my desk in the sunroom...at the back of the house...at the end of the old gravel road.

DO YOU WANT TO KNOW MORE?

Can't wait for the next book in the series? Need to find out what happens next in the life of your favorite character? Want to know more about Dodgeville?

Website:
www.TheOldGravelRoad.com

On this site, I share:

Fun Facts – bite-sized, behind-the-scenes stories

Sneak peeks into the series' progress

Announcements and publication dates

Blog posts about the writing of
The Old Gravel Road book series

Facebook:
www.Facebook.com/TheOldGravelRoad

Instagram:
www.Instagram.com/TheOldGravelRoad

Through both social media platforms you have opportunities to be among the first to know the latest updates within the series. Additionally, here is where you can enter for a chance to win giveaway items related to Dodgeville, SC!

ACKNOWLEDGMENTS

Joe: You and Henry are kindred spirits. Your passion for all things aviation, your strong but gentle spirit, and your love for me came to mind often as I wrote. When you look at the dirty dishes in the sink and say, "Don't worry about those. Go write!" my heart skips a beat. You're my greatest encourager and my best friend. I love you.

Mom (Lorraine Strohbehn): Your eyes may no longer be able to see the written page, but our Thursday morning read-aloud times over the phone between Indiana and South Carolina were something I looked forward to each week. You cheered me on, challenged my mistakes, and changed my thinking on a few of the characters. I am beyond grateful for your help, your support, and your love. I love you bunches and bunches!

My dad (Ben Strohbehn): His battle with Parkinson's ended in 2015, but it taught me much about the disease. He taught me how to fight, even when losing seems inevitable. Parkinson's looks different in each case. It packs a punch. It changes everything. Therefore, I desire to honor my father's memory and to describe the truths I learned and lived through with his Parkinson's as I include its progression throughout this series in the character of Captain Ed Hall.

My siblings, in-laws, nieces, and nephews: You asked how things were going. You read the snippets I sent you and followed up with notes or texts of encouragement. You wore your Dodgeville t-shirts and aprons without a complaint. You kept me going. You were there for me—as you always are. I love you more than the whole wide world and back again.

The followers of *The Old Gravel Road* on social media: You have blown me away by your enthusiasm and eagerness to read this book. You came back, over and over again, to try to win a "Dodgeville" t-shirt or an apron that promoted a book that was still only in the writing stage. Your excitement propelled me forward and kept me writing. Thank you for that and for showing up when you have so many options calling your name.

Though the characters in *The House at the End of the Old Gravel Road* are purely fictional, many were inspired by friends, family members, or small-business owners I highly respect and/or follow or patronize. Therefore, I give a shout-out to the following:

The citizens of Wakarusa and Nappanee, Indiana: You are my Dodgeville, my happy place, and the towns I think of first when I think of home. Your small-town pride fills my mind with memories and my heart with hope. For this, I thank you.

www.Instagram.com/TheHonestHome

Molly's DIY account oozes with creativity and adrenaline; both friends of mine, she and her sister Liz inspired the characters of Decorator Molly and her sister Ellie.

www.wholysmokemauldin.com

James, Lenard, and the tasty food at Wholy Smoke Family Restaurant in Mauldin, SC, inspired many elements within Miss P's Sweet Tea and Sunshine Café. In real life, I have only, only, *only* liked macaroni and cheese from a box. That is, until I tasted the mac and cheese at Wholy Smoke. It's a.ma.zing! Eat there soon...come hungry...thank me later! (I recommend the rib dinner with mac and cheese and peach cobbler as your sides!)

www.parkinson.org

In this series, Bitsy's father, Captain Ed Hall, has Parkinson's. In real life, my father, Ben Strohbehn, had Parkinson's. Our family researched, listened, and did all that we could to learn as much as we could about this disease. The Parkinson's Foundation was one of my greatest resources. Their helpful insights, recommendations, and tools for learning about and dealing with the changes that Parkinson's brings were invaluable. I chose to present Ed Hall's Parkinson's in much the same way, and on the same timeline, in which my father's case presented. Each case is different. That's one of the things that makes Parkinson's tricky. My desire in including this real-life disease in a fictional story is to encourage, help, and support others who may face this or similar life changes within their family.

Of special note: a portion of the proceeds from the royalties from this series will be donated in memory of my father to Parkinson's-related organizations that are seeking to help, encourage, and in various ways support individuals and families impacted by this disease.

ABOUT THE AUTHOR(S)

Bitsy Lee Evans is the name of a fictional blogger whose website is titled *The Old Gravel Road.* Chronicling the antics and backstories of the residents of her small hometown in the Upstate of South Carolina (also fictional), Bitsy draws readers from all around the world. Her live feeds over the Internet are favorites of both young and old. Borrowing from the fictional Dodgeville's town motto, Bitsy describes her writing as a way of providing a safe and cozy place for her readers to come away for a while and be refreshed: "My greatest joy is writing for the enjoyment of others. I want my readers to know that in my stories, *they come first.*"

Brenda Strohbehn Henderson, the creator of these fictional words and locations, draws from her own life stories and from those who have impacted her life to create the characters and settings of Dodgeville, SC. Brenda lives in the Upstate of South Carolina with her husband, retired international airline captain Joe Henderson.

To contact Brenda Strohbehn Henderson:

Mailing address:

Brenda Henderson
634 NE Main St
PO Box 1732
Simpsonville, SC 29681

E-mail:

TheOldGravelRoad@gmail.com

Made in the USA
Coppell, TX
21 July 2021

59257992R00138